NICHOLAS KNIGHT'S
NIGHTSHADE
BOOK 1

DAWN'S TALE

The Nightshade Series, Book 1

NICHOLAS KNIGHT

Burning Bulb
PUBLISHING

Dawn's Tale
By **Nicholas Knight**
Burning Bulb Publishing
P.O. Box 4721
Bridgeport, WV 26330-4721
United States of America
www.BurningBulbPublishing.com

Cover designed by Gary Lee Vincent with the following licensed elements:
- from Fotolia: File: #61150502 | © Tryfonov
- from Fotolia: File: #23997433 | © igorigorevich
- from Fotolia: File: #80628839 | © Lenan
- from iStock: File #59237462 | © JozefKlopacka

First Edition.
Paperback Edition ISBN: 978-0692546604

Printed in the United States of America

DEDICATIONS

For my beloved daughter, Harley Linnette Delorie: You are the best thing that's ever happened to me; my pride and joy, and my only reason for living and not giving up. You forever hold my heart, with no conditions or limits. I love you, and am so sorry that I couldn't be better for you. I wish I could give you reason to be half as proud of me, as I am to be your father. You are the daughter I have always wanted, and my best friend.

For Andrea: I'm sorry I failed at making you love me back. I wish I had what it took to make you want me. We have such a beautiful daughter between us, who deserves so much better than what she got. I know I made some mistakes with you, and I deeply regret them. I also know that I never would have stood a chance at holding on to you, even if I hadn't made those mistakes. Your tastes are too rich for me to satisfy, you're too smart and attractive for me, and pretty much out of my league. I know you never give me a second thought, but I will always love you, even though my feelings will never be returned or reciprocated. I wish I could have been good enough for you, and wish that the three of us could have been a family that wasn't so broken. God bless you.

For my lost but never forgotten soulmate, Erica Linnette Heath: The only one I've ever made love to who honestly loved me back; the only one I've ever been in love with who saw me as worth loving. I'm sorry for giving up on us and for not being there when you needed me the most. I hope you can forgive me for having been such a fool and for losing sight of what truly mattered. I pray that God finds it in His will to give me a second chance with you in Heaven, and that you remember me as I was before I ruined everything. I love you, Erica. I miss you like crazy, and wish you could have known my daughter. (February 22, 1980 - December 27, 2002)

For "Tiger": My orange tabby cat who has never been a pet, but a companion.

For Russell Clayton Harris, Sr. & Russell Clayton Harris, Jr. (my late maternal grandfather and Uncle): Though we were regretfully never close, I feel more connected to you both as I get older, relating more each day to the pain you both suffered in this life. We definitely share a great deal in common, and in many ways are kindred spirits.

For my parents: Thank you for always being there and for never quit caring, in spite of me being a burden and disappointment. I love you both. Thank you for your love and support.

For David & Carolyn: For raising my daughter and for all your kind effort in ensuring that myself and my family can continue to be a part of her life. Thank you both. You mean a lot to me, and I am grateful that Harley has you in her life.

For Jen Bartlebaugh: Thank you for always being such a true friend, even though the cards are stacked against us. You mean so much to me. Thank you for your friendship and for always believing in me. I love you. I look forward to having you as a co-author.

For Chiara Hubner Travezan: For being the primary individual who actually took the time to give me detailed feedback on this story. You're lengthy email did wonders, and helped me improve this novel immensely. Thank you for your time and your notes.

For Gary Lee Vincent: For being so cool and gracious. Thank you for giving me opportunities and chances, which I never would have gotten elsewhere or otherwise. Thank you, from the bottom of my heart, for believing in my novel and me. I owe you, my friend.

OCTOBER 7, 1972

The Simon & Garfunkel song *Bridge Over Troubled Water* overlapped the otherwise dead silence, as the instant classic served as homage to the female super fan laying in the casket at the altar of the local Church of the Nazarene. The funeral mourners paid their respects in their own way, as their thoughts drifted off into personalized reminiscence, even if their cherished memories had suddenly taken artistic license. It was painfully clear that most of the people in attendance were more acquaintances than they had been friends, showing up more for appearance than empathy. There were many males present, who had known the sultry 30-year-old in the Biblical sense, as she hadn't lived in the most honorable way. The tree hugger's promiscuous reputation had earned her several male admirers in Maryland, and her good-looking corpse now laid to rest from her drawn-out and inevitably terminal battle with Lupus.

Though the widower was a beloved evangelical minister, he had the mortician officiate the grim proceedings. He had loved his dead wife, but didn't have words to say about her that would leave her in a good light, and he wanted to be respectful for the sake of those who showed up and his young daughter in particular. Reverend Mingan Moon, however, still got glares of disturbing discontent, as a few people happened to observe and notice him flipping through a comic book that he had discreetly pulled out from underneath his overcoat. *Marvel* had just released a new title called *Werewolf By Night*, and the unhappily married bachelor now held the anticipated first issue in his hands, which were now slightly trembling. His excitement grew even stronger when he stumbled across an ad in the back of the comic, for a life-size inflatable doll. These scowls of disapproval and disgust were a bit hypocritical, as these very same people who were arrogantly judging Reverend Moon, were snacking on 20-cent candy, like Cherry flavored *Cosmic Candy* or Orange flavored *Space Dust*.

There were several varied types of hairstyles accounted for. The younger women had long, straight, and center-parted hair. Others had shorter pageboy, shag and wedge styles. Then some had shoulder-length feather cut hair with flicked out wings around the ears. Somewhat surprisingly, the men wore their hair very similar, if not exactly like the women. These same individuals who would normally be seen decked out in gypsy attire had at least dressed in all-black formal wear to be polite and show courtesy for the deceased.

A 13-year-old olive-skinned girl walked up to the open casket, with salty tears filling her beautiful yet battered, crystal-blue eyes. Dawn's semi Native American complexion was overshadowed by a personalized black cloud, which she would all too soon become very familiar with, as it would hover over her for the rest of her days...which were destined to be filled with turmoil, torment, loss and disappointment. The seventh-grader had arrived in the most formal attire she had at her disposal, which included a pair of khaki corduroy bell-bottoms that had a tribal arrow design stitched and detailed on the back pockets. She also wore a red boiled wool vest with black velvet detail around the fold over collar and armholes with beautiful geometric velvet designs.

Dawn played with the mood ring on her finger, as she reminisced back to the day when her mother pulled over alongside the road, just to snag a lost *Gayla* baby bat keel-guided plastic kite from off a fence post. She then recalled how her Daddy would push little Dawn on the swing at the park, or carry her in his arms while walking through the Zoo or theme park, even when Dawn could tell that it was straining her father's lower back problems. Dawn, unfortunately, also remembered those nights when her mother would bring home various, multiple, strange men, whom she would lead into her marital bed, while Dawn's father was out of the house, often leading a ministry event or counseling one or more of the congregation members or couples. So, as much as Dawn already missed her late but selfish mother, it broke her young heart to remember what a callous whore she was and how she unappreciated and mistreated her father, whom she admired and respected. As Dawn approached the open casket to say her final goodbyes, she reached out and touched her loose mother on the cheek, which she instantly regretted, not expecting or anticipating her skin to be so damn petrified. Though she felt she owed it to her mother to bid a proper farewell, and loved her in spite of the internal damage she had done to her father, it was disheartening for her to see her now be just as cold on the outside.

When Dawn got back to her home in Silver Spring, she went straight to her room, to bury her wet, young face in her fluffy pillow, which had the artistic image of a wolf on the case. As she attempted to cry herself to sleep in the middle of the afternoon, while a mixture of relatives and parishioners were out in the kitchen and living room area, stuffing their faces and chatting about memories past…her Cherokee father came through her door, quietly shut and locked it behind him, and sat down beside her on the bed. A *Creedence Clearwater Revival* LP was playing the song *Bad Moon Rising*, and though her bedroom door was closed, the music and lyrics seeped and vibrated through the somewhat thin walls. The little girl's bedroom was dark, and was divided between Indian artifacts and wall art, and hippy decorations from her deceased flower-child mother.

There was a homemade mobile hanging above her bed, which had wolves running in a circle. Her bed sheets were also equally wolf-themed. As Dawn gazed aimlessly at the silver-based, faded lava lamp, which sat on the nightstand beside her, the 45-year-old man who had helped given her life, took what he felt was owed him.

"You're the apple of my eye, baby," he said to her in a threatening whisper, just loud enough for her ears to hear and her heart to fear. "We're all we have now," he added, as she could hear his breath get faster and heavier, as the hand that once cradled her, slid its clammy palm up the length of the backside of her leg. His breath reeked of a toxic combination of cheap liquor and tobacco. "We need to be there for each other, now that we've lost your mother."

Meanwhile, out in the rest of the house, the unsupervised guests quickly became footloose and fancy-free, as they jived to the record player, and danced together on the shag carpet. Some even made out on the white leather couch in the living room. The guests had gotten over Linda's premature passing fairly early, as their grieving had obviously been short-lived. The house had suddenly evolved into one big party, with *Shasta Cola* cans and *Chiclet* gum boxes thrown and tossed on the floor. The *Zenith* picture-tube color television (that was turned on, but wasn't being watched) played the Woodsy Owl commercial, which nobody paid any attention to, which gave the slogan *Give a hoot, don't pollute.* As the huge speakers blared the rock music, two of the women were busy in the kitchen, preparing some liver and onions for the guests, and while they were letting it cook in the stove, they heated up themselves by getting frisky with each other. The guests, who were still clothed, had changed out of their formal wear and were now sporting long sleeved baseball shirts with iron-on designs of pop-culture, jean vests and short denim skirts, and long knee socks with two horizontal stripes at the top. One of the male guests, who couldn't seem to get laid, took it upon himself to serve as the DJ, switching out the records to give a little more variety to the morbid celebration.

The classic Jim Morrison *Open Arms* poster hung on her wall, which had been a gift from her dead mother. Jim's paper eyes looked down at the tragedy that was occurring before him, as the Cherokee reverend committed the ultimate sin and defiled his own child. Leaning over, he bit her on the butt, before slowly sliding her Days-of-the-Week panties down and off her underage legs. The frightened Dawn just lay there frozen, like a piece of petrified wood, sensing that this wasn't right. She gently shut her tear-filled eyes and imagined that she was running in a strawberry field with her late bohemian mother, laughing and dancing together in their colorful gypsy attire. Her father's sweat smelled like burning incense, as it merely took

"Fuck me!" her incestuous father yelled out, as he just barely stopped himself from falling on his face. "Fuck, Dawn, can't you clean up your room? Have some respect," he said, as the remorseless pedophile kicked her metal *Family Affair* lunchbox across the bedroom. This time, Reverend Moon slammed the door behind him, which nobody even heard, because of the music being so obnoxiously loud.

As Reverend Moon left her alone to sulk in private, Dawn could hear the Bee Gees song *Night Fever* play out in the hallway, while her door was momentarily open. Little Dawn bled over her wolf-decorated sheets that day, while the funeral reception carried on out in the rest of the dysfunctional house. This would be the first of many milestones, or rites of passages, that would warp her into becoming the troubled, disturbed young woman she would grow into. There was a full moon the night that Dawn was robbed of her childhood and innocence. Dawn was broken from harboring the detrimental bitterness and resentment, which developed more over time from the adversity and affliction that had hardened, not humbled, her. Her inability and unwillingness to forgive and forget would inevitably and eventually turn lethal, as her incestuous father and her harlot mother would both determine and define who she would grow to become. As miserable and tormenting as her pain was, at least it never abandoned or betrayed her.

OCTOBER 27, 1977

The cluster of mental misfits gathered together in their usual cliques, as they chose where to sit in the mess area. Nurse Carl walked in and tapped Dawn on the shoulder. Dawn knew what to expect, and though not thrilled about it, had grown numb to her lot in life.

"Hey, Dawn," he said. "I need some help with something. You think you could do me a solid?" Nurse Carl asked, with an evil smirk. She showed hesitance in her pretty face, even though it never seemed to help her stand her ground. "Come with," Nurse Carl said again. "I promise, it'll be a gas." As Dawn reluctantly, but obediently, got out of her chair, she followed him out of the dining area.

William, who wasn't sitting with Dawn, but noticed her all the same, watched her hesitate to leave with Nurse Carl, with worry in his heart and bad thoughts in his head. He perceived that something was amiss, and that Nurse Carl was abusing his authority. He just couldn't prove it. He worried about Dawn.

"Did you guys hear about the new guy?" Chad asked, as he persisted in looking over his shoulder, as if watching someone who wasn't actually there. There wasn't even a window for him to be looking through, but apparently, just an imaginary friend.

"The one that just got admitted earlier tonight?" Kenneth inquired, while he was working on a *Mad Lib*, putting only inappropriate and indecent answers in the blanks, being as crude as possible.

"Yeah," Chad replied. "Did one of you just call me a psycho?" he asked his disturbed, intimate group of peers.

"What?" Kenneth asked. "Nobody called you that, you bozo. What the hell's wrong with you?"

"Isn't this new guy supposed to be a Nazi or something?" Thomas asked.

Meanwhile, Nurse Carl had led Dawn to the utilities closet.

"Go in," Nurse Carl said, as he opened the door for her, not to be a gentleman, but to make sure she listened and followed orders.

Dawn was irresolute, each time she was asked to do this, but she was trained to respect *the Man*, whether it be her fundamentalist minister father, or another esteemed figure of authority. Nurse Carl had mentioned to her several times of his service as a Marine. This was something he bragged about often and profusely, as if to put himself on a pedestal. Though she didn't want to enter the dark closet, she did as she was told. Nurse Carl walked in after her, and shut the door behind him.

"This time," he said, as he began to undo his pants. "I want you to lick my ass clean, before giving me my regular request," he said, as he dropped his pants, and turned his back to Dawn.

"I'm not comfortable with this," she said, in a whimper kind of voice. "And it's not exactly a request, when I don't have a choice."

"Hey," Nurse Carl said back. "Do what you're told, bitch. Besides," he said, "Don't knock it. You just might like it."

"You know that you could get busted for this, right?" Dawn said, trying yet again to say anything to discourage him from continuing this gross abuse of power. "You could go away for a long time."

"Sweetie," he said back. "You're not going to tell anyone, because you know that if you ever do, I will hurt you and your family. I have your file. I know where you live. I have your social security number. I know all I need to know about you. Besides, who do you think they're going to believe?"

Dawn put her nose to his droopy, hairy ass, and reluctantly stuck her tongue out in his rancid crack, while her hands were flat on the ground, and she tightly shut her eyes...as she pretended she was anywhere but there. It was significantly difficult to avoid getting his ass hairs entangled and entwined in the small, round, silver stud that she wore just below her left nostril.

"No, no," Nurse Carl stopped her. "Take your hands and spread my cheeks, so you can actually lap my butt hole with your tongue."

While Dawn remained knelt before her perverted elder, she had flashbacks of the sexual abuse she had endured from her evangelical father, who at least didn't smell as rank as Carl did. As Dawn spread him apart, and did as she was instructed, Nurse Carl reminded her of the first rule, which he had clearly established in the beginning.

"Oh, this is so wicked, man! That's better...eat that shit, you naughty girl," he said, showing his seal of approval of how she was doing. "Now remember, don't you stop until I tell you it's time," he said.

Then, as she regretfully cringed and continued to please him with the forced rim job, she felt his anus push outward, as he laid a gasser in her mouth. She immediately pulled away from him, disgusted, spitting on the floor, and wiping her tongue with her hand, which didn't help, as her hand had touched the filthy floor, where she was alongside the bedpans and dustbins.

"Please," she begged him, "No more. That was raunchy."

Carl just tittered, amused with himself.

"What do you expect from an old fart?" he said, laughing at her disparagingly. "Listen, bitch...I served this country. Now, you're going to serve me."

Carl then turned around, and grabbed her by the hair, pulling her to him, so that her face was now in his bushy groin.

"I thought I told you not to stop until I said it was okay?" he said. "I'm going to have to punish you now. Suck it," he demanded, "and this time, deep throat it."

Again, she did as she was told, while this coerced undertaking killed her inside a little more each time.

"That's it. Suck it hard," he said. "Yank my chain too, while you're sucking it," the crude RN told her, as he gyrated back and forth, as if humping her mouth.

Without warning, Carl shoved his well-endowed manhood all the way in her mouth, and held her head in place, to keep her from letting up on it.

"That's it mama," he said in his sinister voice, "In your face! Suck it to the bone."

Dawn frantically slapped, and pushed against, the side of his Neanderthal legs, trying everything she could to get him to let go of her head, but he refused to release her. She began choking, and her face started to turn blue. She had made herself relax her throat, but it didn't help. She couldn't breathe. Nurse Carl finally let her go, causing her to collapse on the floor, wheezing and gasping for air.

"That's a good doggy," Nurse Carl told her, "Perhaps you'll listen better next time."

Back in the ward's cafe, William found it difficult to continue eating, while he genuinely feared for Dawn's welfare.

"He's German, retard. Not all Germans are Nazis," Kenneth corrected.

"Yeah. They're not like Muslims," William chimed in, "There are such a thing as good Germans."

"There's good Muslims," Kenneth insisted, shocking the others that he had moments of marginal empathy, though he was usually known to be brutally prejudice and set in his ways.

"Dig it, there's different kinds of Muslims. They're not all the same," Chad agreed with the superior-acting heavyweight.

"Yeah, the Moonies and the Shit-Tights," Thomas said, being entirely mistaken but completely serious.

"No, doofus, the Sunni and the Shiite," Kenneth corrected yet again.

"Oh," Thomas said. "Hey, don't touch my plate," he told Kenneth, who happened to have his hand on the table, but nowhere near Thomas's personal space. "I don't want to catch your germs," the neurotic hypochondriac stressed.

"Dream on," William cut in, "They have different branches, and each claim to have their own special creed, but the plain truth is, all Muslims follow the same manual. Have you ever read the Quran? There are verses on practically every page, about how the infidel should be treated. There is no such thing as radical Islam, when they all faithfully abide by the same hateful book. In the case of the Nazis, it was much different. The Nazis based their beliefs on more than one religion, and were, ironically enough, heavily influenced by Islam."

"Really?" Chad asked, never hearing that explained that way before, still looking behind him, as if he was seeing something, or someone only he could see.

"Oh yeah," William reiterated, "Hitler was a huge admirer of their pedophile prophet, Muhammad. Hitler was very much inspired by the Quran. Do your research. It's historical fact."

"Aren't all religions basically the same anyway, though?" Chad asked.

"Really? Name one other religion that will butcher your entire family if you do so much as dare draw a picture of their prophet. Name one other religion that will behead you if you leave the faith," William challenged.

"They say that Islam is a religion of peace," Thomas noted.

"Sure," William agreed. "There's a piece of you over here, and a piece of you over there."

"You're just racist," Kenneth directly accused.

"Seriously?" William challenged. "Tell me how exactly I am racist, for speaking out against a religion. Islam is a theology, not an ethnicity."

"I feel like scoring some dope," Thomas said, changing the subject.

"Me too," Chad agreed, "I could dig getting stoned."

"If you two were Muslim brides, you would be," William shared. "Muslims stone their women, and their daughters, sometimes to the death, for doing nothing more than disobeying or disagreeing with them, no matter how trivial or petty the offense."

"If you wake up and you don't want to smile," Chad began to bust out in spontaneous song, sensing that the topic, and direction of their heavy conversation had gotten way too deep for their collective, fragile state of mind.

"If it takes just a little while," Thomas jumped in, and began singing along with Chad, while moving and bouncing his head from side to side, shaking his fro hairstyle.

"Open your eyes and look at the day, you'll see things in a different way," the two of them sang in unison.

William noticed Dawn coming back to her empty seat, and saw that her hair had been messed up, and that the look on her face was less than far out. His troubled eyes watched her with sincere concern, certain that there was something wrong, that she just wasn't confiding.

"Don't stop thinking about tomorrow," Chad sang louder.

"Don't stop, it'll soon be here," one of the less masculine-looking female nurses sang, chiming in, as she strolled by their table. "It'll be here, better than before."

"Yesterday's gone, yesterday's gone," Chad and Thomas sang in sync.

Joshua hears them singing the *Fleetwood Mac* song, and gets up from his table, and begins to dance with exuberance. He twirls around the room, as if he's a human merry go round, flaying his arms about, and flapping his limp wrists in his prideful display of gayness.

"Why not think about times to come," William suddenly helped out, keeping the song going, and actually drumming on the table with his hands.

"And not about the things that you've done," Chad sang.

"If your life was bad to you," Thomas added.

"Just think what tomorrow could do," all three harmonized together.

"Loving you, isn't the right thing to do," Kenneth started singing, not only poorly off tune, but singing the wrong song by the same band, rudely interrupting their tribute recital, and receiving a dirty look from the three of them, for doing so. Though no music had been playing right then, the psychiatric ward did have access to a LP record player, and had a modest selection of vinyl albums, which they kept handy behind the counter, mostly donated by the various staff members. Periodically, the RN on duty would put on a *Bread* album, or something equally soft and soothing, for the patients to enjoy.

Chad looked over at the table where Bethany and Benjamin were eating alone together, and saw that they were staring at them, with a mutual look of silent insult on their faces. Their eyebrows were raised, chins lowered, and smiling out of the corner of their mouths. Bethany had a chronic phobia of other people, and only felt comfortable with Benjamin. Benjamin suffered from a vast lack of enthusiasm and eagerness to participate in any sort of activity. He was also quiet and a bit on the anorexic side.

"What?" Chad asked, feeling he did the right thing by trying to change the unseen, yet highly noticeable, editorial mood ring in the room.

Elsewhere in the asylum, Reuben came to, and discovered himself in the cramped, padded room. His dry eyes, as usual, were infected with the grittiness and burning, that he had learned to live with, but never quite got accustomed to.

He finds himself in nothing but a diminutive hospital gown, which just barely covers his 41-year-old scrotum, which had shrunk some but fortunately not dropped yet. The gown was bleached white, like the room he was now confined in against his will. The gown appeared to be made of fabric, but was grossly thinner and somehow significantly more uncomfortable than a roach-motel, soiled bed sheet.

The solid, untainted white blanketed everything in sight that is what little there was to actually see. The room looked more like a prison cell, than a hospice chamber. There is no mirror, which Reuben obviously didn't miss. There was a small, square window, in the upper part of the door.

In the higher corner of the wall, beside the door, was a small speaker, which was playing the song *Have You Ever Been Mellow* by Olivia Newton-John, on a repetitive loop. The documented theory was that the soothing music was to keep the new patient calm and collected, in a relaxed state. However, off the record, it was obvious that it was intended to be a nuisance, and even a trigger of sorts, to unofficially keep the patient unstable, and therefore selfishly secure the continued insurance and outrageous funding that they were criminally draining from the naive newcomer.

Reuben begins to notice that someone comes by and glances in the window, with an obnoxiously bright flashlight, every fifteen minutes or so. It's never the same person twice, and they consistently chose their checks to coincide with the precise moments when Reuben decided to look in that direction, thereby ensuring that their detrimental, battery-operated beacon hits him directly in the eyes each time.

Reuben's eyes were photosensitive, so he bawled in agony, as the hazardous lamp tormented him. There were no restraints or shackles on his wrists or ankles, but there was also nothing in the room which he could use to harm himself or others. He had been committed, and was now undergoing an initial observation period, yet had absolutely no recollection of how he got there.

Reuben stares down at his scrawny forearms, which he had recently carved up with a partially rusted fillet knife. His self-inflicted lacerations had been effectively sterilized and stitched, but the red linear marks were still raucous, particularly against his pale, albino flesh. Reuben was in a psychiatric ward, which was a semi-heavily secured facility within a much larger hospital, in Falls Church, VA.

Dawn lounged and slouched in the smoking room, deliberately isolating herself from the others, just to take a break from having to keep up her charade, hiding the burden she carried and buried inside. The designated room was enclosed by durable Plexiglas, and just adjacent to the solarium, where most of the patients were sedated on the long, 6-piece, floral-patterned sectional sofa, either aimlessly watching television, or dazed in deep personal reflection. Dawn took her time puffing on one Marlboro cigarette, but only until the coast was clear. Once she verified that nobody was close enough to catch her or narc on her, she sat back on the wooden bench, and pulled out a small, silver flask, which she kept concealed in a zippered fanny pack, that she had strapped around her waist. This was one of the many gifts and privileges she indulged, courtesy of the perverted, male staff members who coveted her. In exchange for sexual favors, these depraved, entrusted guardians provided her with a supply of illegal moonshine, which she kept tucked away in her room. Though her flirtatious, extrovert behavior would never show it, the dense liquor was for much more than simply taste. She was dispirited and forlorn, and it engulfed her very being, like a flood. She desperately needed something substantial and meaningful to fill her void, and not just her feminine cavities.

Meanwhile, Reuben nearly rubbed his face raw, with his naturally chilled and clammy hands. His empty despair and absolute desolation overwhelmed his forsaken soul, but yet no tears flowed from his pitiful and dismal eyes. He had wept so much, and so often, that he had literally exhausted his reservoir. Reuben suffered from porphyria, a rare and incurable blood disease, which sadistically attacked his body in a myriad of ways. His debilitated teeth were yellowed, and jagged, as if they were all decaying incisors. His ulcer-gingivitis afflicted gums had retracted to the point where his teeth looked much longer than normal.

Though it appeared that he had fangs, his enamel was actually eroding, and he only made it worse by his subconscious tendency to grind them. He didn't remember signing into the hospital, or being asked questions about what had happened to him. He figured these things must have occurred, but that he had just blacked them out.

Bethany was in the solarium, amusing herself by playing the theme music to *Ryan's Hope* on her cherished bamboo flute, which she had found months ago in one of the common areas, and had developed an oddly emotional attachment to. While most in the room were off in their own imaginary worlds, and unbothered by her performance, there was one intolerant patient who found this to be incredibly annoying, as he was actually trying to watch the soap opera of the same name.

"Will you shut the hell up?!" the obese, yet arrogant Kenneth said, infuriated with the rude interference.

Dawn had walked in, just in time to overhear Kenneth verbally intimidating Bethany's musical recital.

"Buzz off, Kenny," Dawn insisted.

"Who's going to make me?" Kenneth retorted in what he perceived to be justified retaliation to Bethany's discourteous behavior.

"Listen, Kenny. We all know you're here because of anger issues, but you really need to learn to pick on someone at least half your own size," Dawn said bravely.

"You have a big mouth, Dawn," he said in response, feeling insulted by who he viewed as inferior. "You must need to put something in it," he added, referring to his tiny reproductive organ that he hadn't actually seen in what felt like a lifetime.

Dawn quickly brought her hand to her mouth, and when she neglected to respond immediately, Kenneth misinterpreted that as a victory.

"What's a matter, baby?" he asked, "Cat got your tongue?"

"Sorry. No. I just threw up in my mouth a little," Dawn responded.

"That's the last straw!" Kenneth said, wobbling up from the sofa, which had a permanent crater-sized indentation from where his blubber butt was parked. Waddling over to where Dawn was standing, behind the modular sofa, he now faced his attacker. "I'm going to teach you a lesson," he said, clenching his fat fists, and panting for air.

Dawn made a noise, under her breath that was faint but fierce, which sounded like a growling.

"Look everybody," Kenneth said in mirth, "this chick thinks she's a wolf."

"Actually, the wolf is my animal totem," Dawn said back, with a vivid death wish in her dangerous eyes.

Just then, Nurse Claire stepped in, and broke it up.

"That's right," Dawn called out to Kenneth, who was tottering back to his room, "Keep truckin!"

Bethany still hadn't budged an inch, deathly afraid of Kenneth's hostile demeanor.

"Are you okay, Bethany?" Dawn asked, walking up to her, to make sure she was alright.

Just then, Benjamin came walking in, hearing the ruckus from the hallway. He walked over to where the two girls were standing.

"What's going on?" Benjamin asked Dawn, seeing that Bethany was temporarily paralyzed in fear. "Is she okay?" he asked again, in a panic. "Bethany, are you okay?" he asked his friend directly, no longer waiting for a response from Dawn.

Dawn didn't know how to answer Benjamin; so instead, she reached out to touch Bethany's shoulder, as her way of communicating to her that she was safe.

"No!" Benjamin stopped her, "Don't. She doesn't like to be touched."

Not wanting to make matters worse than they already were, Dawn put her hand down, being stopped just in time, before she had made physical contact.

"It's alright, Bethy," Benjamin said, as he petted the back of Bethany's hair, ever so gently, as if trying to calm her down. "Don't trip out. Everything's alright."

"T-t-thank you," Bethany said, "Th-th-thank you, Dawn, for m-m-making him go away," she stammered, as Dawn had already begun to leave the scene, missing out on Bethany's verbal expression of gratitude.

Reuben battled his inner demons, aggressively covering his ears with his hands, like a severely autistic child, as he struggled to force the evil images out of his troubled head. He blinked heavily and repeatedly, incapable of properly handling the stress and anxiety that came with being him. The brick walls, which had been painted solid white, only served as a blank page for the Devil to fill with unwanted, unwelcome thoughts of self-destruction. To his dismay, there was nothing at his current disposal that could assist him in harming himself. The bed had no wires or springs, no headboard to tie to, and no linens to form a noose. There was no ceiling fan or nightstand, telephone or television. There was no lamp, or light fixture. In fact, the only light source came from the little window on the securely fastened, heavily scrutinized door.

For the first time, Dawn occupied the solarium unaccompanied; as the other patients had either already retired for the night, or were busy visiting their families. It was that time of the month, where patients were permitted to have a brief, thirty-minute visitation with pre-approved relatives. This meant that the visitors were required to prove with documented identification that they fit the denotation of immediate family, meaning parents, siblings, children, or grandparents. These visits weren't that enjoyable, as the visitors were forced to endure strict and grueling preparation, before being allowed inside. They were patted down, and everything on (and in) their body, was thoroughly inspected and evaluated. These visits were also supervised, which made them awkward and apprehensive for everyone involved. Fortunately, Dawn didn't have to deal with this part of the psychiatric incarceration, as she wasn't about to invite any of her family to come see her. In fact, when she was originally committed, she was given the option of putting her father on the approved list, and chose to decline and surrender that right.

Dawn Moon had run away from home several months back, and her family members were completely in the dark on where she was or what had happened to her. She was embarrassed to be in the psychiatric unit, but not as much as she was about her last name. Her father had molested her regularly and routinely, since her mother's sudden passing five years prior. He was an ordained minister, and a respected chief in his Indian tribe. Her mother had been a free-loving, earth-worshipping hippie, who had a particular fetish for the Native American culture.

Dawn spent the last couple free hours of the evening, in front of the tubular television. She was watching a new, highly publicized, primetime show on NBC called *CHiPs*, about two California motorcycle patrolmen. As Dawn celebrated this rare, isolated opportunity with a few more swigs of her treasured silver flask, it occurred to her that it was unbefitting and perplexing that the room was professionally referred to as a solarium, when there were no translucent walls, and no solar radiation penetrating the room during daytime.

Dawn had reclined in the solarium several times before, but never noticed until now, that there were potted plants in the corners, hanging from the ceiling. They looked to be dying from neglect. The intercom called for *lights out*, and the last of the patients returned to their rooms, while the shift change made its rotation among the staff.

Reuben stayed up for hours, too edgy and uncomfortable to relax, as he watched the various nurses check in on him, almost too often. He manically scratched his prominent sideburns, like he was a house cat who had gotten into his junkie-owner's stash of psychedelic acid. Eventually, Reuben caved in, and dosed off, not looking forward to the next day, which he was confident would bring only more of the same.

Sometime after midnight, Reuben had a disconcerting nightmare, which concluded with him waking up in a glass coffin, in an open grave, in the blazing heat of summer. A crowd of Catholic clergymen gathered around the border of the dug hole, and concurrently pissed blood all over the pellucid lid, while Reuben blared out the words, "Wait, I'm not dead!" over and over.

OCTOBER 28, 1977

Nurse Gregory awaked Reuben just after sunrise.

"Mr. Peterson?" Nurse Gregory called, standing in the doorway of the observation cell. "Mr. Peterson? Wake up!"

Reuben's eyes still stung with watery discharge. Prior to his compulsory registration, Reuben had been long accustomed to sleeping all day, and being up all night. He was definitely more of a night owl, which didn't seem to coincide well with this new, undesirable situation. Reuben reluctantly opened his eyes, at least the best he could, and made eye contact with the Hispanic male nurse.

"Rise and shine amigo," Nurse Gregory said, "Come on. Get up. You're probation period is over, man."

Reuben's introductory period of constant surveillance had ended. He was escorted to another room, furnished with regular walls and a door that he could use at his leisure. The downside was, he would have to share this space with another male patient.

Reuben wasn't keen on the roommate idea, considering his outer shell. Reuben preferred isolation, even alienation, as the outsider had accepted early on that his future only promised rejection and abhorrence.

The room offered a set of bunk beds, and two small, painted white, wooden nightstands, which had two drawers inside each of them. There was a single shelf just above each nightstand that was both attached to the wall with brackets and screws. This room served as a breath of fresh air, compared to the gloomy cell he had reluctantly stayed overnight in.

He did notice, however, that there were still no linens on the beds, but only bare mattresses. The room did at least have a light switch, which operated a wall sconce, which was dim, but substantial. Reuben was given a care package, which included a bar of *Dial* soap, a tube of *Ultra Brite* toothpaste, two bath towels, and two sets of unfashionable uniforms, which were a depressing shade of baby blue. He was also given a pair of fluffy slippers, which matched the uniforms. There was also a wallet-sized, laminated calendar in the package, which laid out the weekly schedule for Reuben, all of which was mandatory.

"I noticed there isn't a toothbrush in here, but there's toothpaste?" he inquired to the seemingly steroid-injected male nurse.

Nurse Gregory noticed Reuben's thick German accent.

"When you're ready to brush your teeth each night, you may request a toothbrush and one razor, from the nurse's desk," Gregory explained, in a monotone voice, as if reading off a Q-card. "One of us will then chaperone you to the communal bathroom, and observe you until you're finished, at which point you will be expected to return the toothbrush and the razor to us, by disposing it in a trash bag which we will be holding open for you."

"You watch us, while we're using the bathroom?" Reuben asked, distraught at this unsettling revelation.

"Only while you are in possession of those items," Nurse Gregory corrected, as if to attempt to either comfort him or to conceal the facility's perverted intentions.

"Still," Reuben continued, "I wouldn't exactly call it a dynamite policy. It seems to me that it's a clear violation of our rights."

"Mr. Peterson, let me give you the lowdown...you've been committed into a mental hospital. You have no rights anymore," Nurse Gregory told the physical aberration, "At least not while you're still with us."

Just then, Reuben's appointed roommate casually entered the room. His hair and face were damp, and had a towel wrapped around his waist, as if it hadn't occurred to him to bring his clothes along with him, when he made the trip to the communal shower. He had straight short hair, combed to the side, thick sideburns, and a bushy mustache. His bunkmate appeared to be about ten years younger than him, as he coldly brushed by Reuben, without even acknowledging his presence. He whistled ambiguously, while proceeding to shamelessly drop his towel, and put his spare uniform on, in front of both Reuben and Nurse Gregory.

"Reuben, this is Joshua," Nurse Gregory introduced them, sensing that it clearly wasn't going to happen otherwise. "Joshua, why don't you say hello to Reuben? You're going to be bunkmates for the duration of your stay here," Nurse Gregory continued to try and help Reuben start off well in his new quarters.

Joshua still offered no response or recognition that they were even in the room, but in fact blatantly ignored them at every turn. Reuben looked at Nurse Gregory and communicated, with his eyes, that he wasn't happy with the situation, to say the least. Nurse Gregory, though not obligated in his job description to do so, went the extra mile, as he could see that Reuben didn't deserve this.

"Reuben," he said, "Um, can I speak to you for a moment out here? I forgot to go over a couple of things with you."

"Slammin," Reuben agreed, putting on phony enthusiasm, to hide his ever-growing depression.

Reuben stepped out of his new claustrophobic habitat, and Nurse Gregory shut the door behind them, leaving the narcissistic Joshua to himself.

"Listen, vato," Nurse Gregory began, "I'm sorry to have to put you with him. If you haven't noticed, Joshua is kind of a drag. He isn't exactly the friendliest patient here in the ward."

"Yeah," Reuben nodded, "That seems to be an understatement."

"Yeah, well, unfortunately, they don't give me much authority here. I have to follow orders, like you guys. But, if it's any consolation to you, you're welcome to come to me, if you need someone to talk to, or if you have any questions or complaints."

"Thanks," Reuben said, "I appreciate that."

"Yeah, well, I know this has to be hard. I can't imagine how I would handle being trapped in a mental prison like this. Look, gabacho, most of the male nurses here are loco and have their own self-serving agendas, but I was raised to have a little more compassion for people."

"I can dig it, Nurse Gregory," Reuben said, reading the nurse's nametag. "Thank you. I'm Reuben, by the way. Just call me Reuben."

"Gregory Gabino," Nurse Gregory said, shaking Reuben's hand. "You'll be alright, Reuben. Hang in there, okay?" he added, patting Reuben on the shoulder, "Don't let this situation get you down. You just have to keep on keepin' on. Watch out for some of these female nurses here. Most of them are puta la judas."

The chicano RN walked away, leaving Reuben to get acquainted with his new standoffish cohabitant. Reuben was basically a recluse, and wasn't gregarious in the least. He had no interest in pursuing social interaction with anyone. He just stood there and watched, as Joshua flamboyantly pranced around the room, as if he were sequestered in a vivid rainbow of seclusion. It didn't take long for Reuben to deduce that Joshua was gleefully queer, which suddenly made Reuben even more grateful that Joshua had no desire to engage in conversation or interaction with him. Where Joshua seemed to be perfectly content, Reuben grew more paranoid by the minute that he was destined to be maladjusted in his new unwanted surroundings.

Breakfast wasn't anything special, and just barely edible, even for those who didn't share his cursed allergies. The paper plate consisted of flaky, scrambled eggs, a single buttered biscuit, and a side of bunk canned potatoes. Everything on the plate was pointlessly and copiously saturated in a heavy, garlic flavored syrup. Reuben speared the biscuit with the plastic fork, thinking that it might be the one thing that he could manage to salvage. As he raised it off the plate, he watched as the greasy mixture poured back onto the plate, which literally drowned in lard and chemicals. The quality of the food was just below the toxic waste they serve children in American public schools. Reuben looked in detested aversion, as the glycerin-based poison dripped off the side of the flimsy, unstable plate. The ginger outcast wondered how long he'd need to go hungry, as he was thankful that the plates were already set out, before the patients were convened.

Reuben had strategically chosen a table on the end, where no one else had occupied. Though he hunched, hung his head, and tried his best to be invisible, he could feel the collective stare throughout the room. Reuben wished he had a smokescreen that he could make magically appear, to cloak him from the all-too-familiar loathing he felt in the room full of condemning, superficial strangers. He suddenly missed the unbearable loneliness he had felt at home; as it was far better than the shallow disgust he received now.

A thick, butch female nurse came around and administered pills to all the patients in attendance. No words were spoken and no directions were given, but it was implied that these pills were to be taken, and that objectionable consequences would follow if they were refused.

"What is this?" Reuben dauntlessly inquired.

"Can it and take it, the nasty nurse demanded sternly, denying him the courtesy of an answer, "You have to take one every morning. No questions."

"I don't think it's too much to ask, to know what I'm swallowing...Nurse Claire, is it?" Reuben added, reading the name off her identity pin.

"Look, sir, if you don't take it, I will be more than happy to call Nurse Carl over. Trust me, you'll take it then. This can happen the easy way or the hard way. Makes no difference to me. No skin off my back, either way."

"Fine," Reuben said, "I'll take it."

Reuben had no intention of taking the pill, but figured it best to lead her on and humor her, so that she would stop nagging him. Reuben went back to poking at his grotesque plate of poison, when he noticed that she wasn't leaving.

"Do I look like a maroon to you?" she asked, "Do I look like a deadhead? I wasn't born yesterday, and I don't reside in La La Land with the rest of you. You take it now, in front of me," she demanded, giving Reuben a sinister look and making damn sure he could see it.

Reuben was hesitant for a moment, but knew if he caused her blood pressure to escalate any further, she would spread the word that he was a troublemaker, and therefore make his stay there even more miserable.

"Okay, Nurse Claire. Sorry I didn't listen," he said as he popped the pill in his mouth, and took a drink from his Dixie cup, "It won't happen again."

"That's better," Nurse Claire retorted. "I should hope this wouldn't be a problem again. Chill, the medication will make you feel good."

Reuben waited a few minutes after Nurse Claire had walked away, and once he knew she was out of view, he quickly reached in his mouth and retrieved the pill from underneath his tongue. Holding it under the table, between his thighs, he crushed it into dust with his deformed fingers. As agitated as the homely Nurse Claire had made him, he was strangely relieved to see that she didn't respond at all to his monstrous looks. As he finished the last of his paper cup of artificially concentrated Apple Juice, he heard the soothing, captivating voice of a seductress. Looking up, he saw a longhaired brunette, much younger than himself, walking into the cafeteria. Her hair flowed behind her, effortlessly and gracefully, as if stepping into a beach breeze.

"Hubba hubba," Reuben said to himself, just under his breath, as he tried not to drool over this missing angel of Heaven.

She was chatting with both staff and patients, as if she was comfortably at home and completely upbeat about her plate. Everyone quit staring at Reuben and shifted their full attention to this stunning vision, which was refreshing for him to have the spotlight placed on someone other than himself. She was beyond beautiful, and could have put every go-go dancer to shame.

Reuben was the only one who didn't drool or fawn over her, at least not publicly. Her uniform pants were pulled down a bit, as to show the tip of her ass cleavage. Every guy in the room took notice of this visual gift right away, and wasn't about to utter a word of protest.

"That's it, mama," Chad said, just under his breath, "Let it all hang out."

She was late to breakfast, yet nobody seemed to mention or dispute it. Reuben tried hard not to scope her, but this became increasingly difficult. Even though everyone else in the mock cafeteria had stared at him, she didn't seem to notice. Though he would have liked her to see him, he was grateful that she didn't, as not gaining her attention was much less painful than her anticipated disgust. Reuben watched the girl of his wet dreams sit at one of the more populated tables, noticing that she hadn't gotten herself any food, but just a Dixie cup of the cheap quality apple juice.

"Hey, Dawn," William said, "What's shakin'?"

"Hey William," she said back, "How's it hanging?"

William blushed, and politely excused himself, not spiritually comfortable in answering that personal question…at least not honestly.

Chad, who could never take his eyes off her bitchin' rump, thought about her ass shaking up and down, back at his pad, while imagining doing her doggy style.

"Hey, Dawn," Thomas said, "What's poppin'? How do you feel?" he asked, expecting some bad news, as usual.

"I feel fine," Dawn replied.

"Yeah," Chad added, "I bet you do."

"Chad," William cut in, "Be cool."

"I didn't do anything," Chad declared.

"That was uncalled for," William judged, trying to pose as if he were above lusting after a vision like Dawn, or at least having the self-control to refrain from making such sexual comments or hidden implications.

"I don't know what you're talking about," Chad said, getting unnerved. "I didn't say anything demeaning or derogatory to her. In fact, I didn't even undress her...I mean address her," Chad said, completely oblivious that he had said what he had said aloud, in response to Thomas's initial question.

William and Thomas both simultaneously watched Dawn, with genuine concern in their eyes, afraid that she was on a slippery slope towards self-destruction, because of her traumatic history. They only knew bits and pieces about her past, from what little she had shared with them, but they had enough pieces to be able to put it together that whatever had happened to her had definitely defined her. She was bitter and desensitized. Though it was no secret among the residents and staff, that Dawn had a reputation in the funny farm, those who cared to see the tormented soul in her optical windows knew that there was much more to her beneath the surface.

Meanwhile, at a different table, another conversation was taking place, about the new recruit.

"So, what do you make of that new guy?" Bethany asked, once again sitting alone with her sole friend, Benjamin. "Kind of an eerie looking fry, isn't he?" She asked her gentle, but dull companion. "He's no Robby Benson, that's for sure."

"I don't know?" Benjamin answered, not interested, as usual, "but, I wouldn't want to mess with him, or bump into him in a dark alley" he added, agreeing that the new guy looked creepy. Like Reuben, Benjamin just poked at his unsavory food, with his plastic spoon, afraid to eat anything on his greasy plate. "This is so grody," Benjamin said, "Why do they have to smother all of our food in this thick, garlic syrup?"

"Garlic is good for you," Bethany answers, "They say it's supposed to be healthy for your heart."

"Well," Benjamin began, "While I get that, I think they're talking about fresh cloves, not this bogue, artificial, imitation syrup."

"I liked what they served us last night," Bethany said. "I liked the toast points."

"You know they just take slices of white bread and shove them in muffin tins with the corners sticking out, and then toast it in the oven until they're golden brown," Benjamin explained. "When they come out, they are like little cups that stand on their own, and that's how they filled them with the SOS last night."

"Yeah," Bethany said, "That creamed chipped beef was good, but I really prefer it when it's filled with Chicken a la King," she said, licking her lips, "My mother used to make it with mushrooms. She made really good zucchini bread too. She'd cook this Flower Pot Bread, with raisins, and our family would dip it in this cheese Fondue."

"Bethany," Benjamin said, irritated that his friend is making him hungry for some real food. "Are you listening to me? We're being handed bunk meals here," he said. "I wouldn't be surprised if they start giving us a steady diet of stale *Zagnut* bars and cold *SpaghettiOs*."

Kenneth, who had special permission to sit on a recliner (since he was much too heavy for the regular chairs), was holding his finished plate out in front of him, and turning it all kinds of ways, so that he could clean every drop of grease and lard off his plate, with his equally repugnant tongue. Kenneth scarfed down every last bit of grub from his plate, but wasn't nearly satisfied.

"Anyone who doesn't want their food," Kenneth asked aloud, "I'm happy to take it. I could eat gobs of this shit," he said, as if talking to himself, as well as to the others.

Reuben noticed that Joshua had eaten everything off his plate, but that he was staring at it now, with an intense focus, as if he were a pyrokinetic, trying to set the plate aflame with his eyes.

When the patients were told to bring their paper plates to the designated trash bins, Reuben had to very carefully and cautiously carry his full plate, which kept him from this opportunity to talk to her, which he was too nervous to do anyway. Reuben moved up in line, as he watched the unexpected object of his desire walk away to her room. He paid close attention to what room she stopped in front of and went in, so he'd know where to find her later. When Reuben finally got up to the trash bins, Nurse Monica was standing behind the bins, to make sure the patients disposed of their trash properly and respectfully. She immediately observed that Reuben hadn't eaten anything off of his plate.

"What's the matter," Nurse Monica asked him, "Don't you dig our food?"

Reuben looked up at her. She, much unlike Nurse Claire, was very easy on the eyes. That being said, however, she was no match for the much younger brunette that Reuben had instantly fallen into hopeless infatuation with, who could have easily led the sexual revolution all on her own.

"Uhh," Reuben tried to respond to Nurse Monica's question, but although he had heard her speak to him, he completely missed out on what she had said, as his focused mind was clearly elsewhere.

"I suggest you either clean your plate from now on, or skip breakfast next time," she said, "They frown on wasting food here."

"Yes mam," Reuben said back. "Ten-four," he said, this time comprehending and retaining what came out of her pretty mouth.

Dawn was alone in her room, with the door closed. She had been craving some moonshine, like a starved alcoholic, and had left her cherished flask under her mattress.

Reuben spotted her sometime later that afternoon, using one of the common phones. The patients were permitted to make local calls only, and could only do so once a day. The calls were monitored and recorded, which kept the majority of patients away from using the phones at all. The rule was that the calls were to last no more than ten minutes, but this policy was roundly ignored, unless a RN happened to catch you chatting longer, at which point you were made to immediately hang up.

Reuben didn't have anyone to call, but was more than content, just watching her use the phone. This time, she did notice him. She caught him staring at her. But, to his surprise, she didn't appear to mind. In fact, she smiled at him briefly, but benevolently, before returning to concentrating on her phone conversation.

Reuben, embarrassed but relieved, was about to briskly walk away and out of sight, when he noticed that Dawn was recklessly rocking back in the chair, that she had pulled up to the phone. Just as Reuben noticed this, she suddenly lost her balance and began to fall backward. Reuben instinctively rushed over to her aide and caught the back of her chair before it hit the ground. As soon as Reuben had brought he rack up to safety, Dawn turned around in her chair to thank him, but he was gone.

"Hello? Hello? Dawn?" the male voice called out on the other end of the phone, which now hung and swung back and forth against the wall, on the spiral cord. Dawn leaned forward, reached over and picked up the phone, after once again looking over her shoulder to see if she spotted her fleeting rescuer.

It was time for Reuben to meet his assigned therapist. He would see this man every day, for an hour's session of one-on-one counseling.

"Please," the psychiatrist began, "have a seat. I'm Doctor Aaron. I will be your shrink and social worker. Tell me why you're here."

"I don't know," Reuben answered honestly.

"Tell me why you think you're here."

"As I said, I don't know. I have no idea how I got here, or who checked me in, or who undressed me...and put me in that..."

"Your mother brought you in, Mr. Peterson," the doctor interrupted, "She told us that she found you cutting yourself with an unsanitary fillet knife, over the upstairs sink, when you didn't answer her call for supper. She said she gave you the option of submitting to this treatment, or being arrested."

Dr. Aaron found it disturbing, and somewhat pathetic, that this grown man still resided with his parents, and that they still treated him like a child, not knowing the full story behind Reuben's health situation, or even caring about the reasons why.

"Is there someone I can consult with regarding the meals here?" Reuben asked. "I couldn't eat breakfast, because of my food allergy to garlic."

"When you checked in, a nurse took a basic medical history, mostly focusing on medical conditions you currently have that we might have to treat, and a rather more in depth mental health history, including what medications you've taken, what diagnoses you've gotten, and what therapists you've gone to and when. They asked you about dietary restrictions as well," Dr. Aaron explained.

"Well, one, as I explained already, I have no recollection of any of that happening. Two, if they did ask me about my dietary restrictions, it was clearly for no readily apparent reason, given the obvious fact that the cooks do not seem to hear about them or care to respect them," Reuben said in a sarcastic tone, but seriously trying to make a valid point. "I certainly would have mentioned my serious aversion to garlic, which your staff bathed my breakfast in this morning."

"Mr. Peterson," the doctor began again, "What insurance are you using to pay for your treatment here?"

"I don't have any health coverage, none that I've been informed of anyway," Reuben replied.

"I see. So, unless your parents are insanely rich, and have a ton of bread, which I haven't seen any evidence of, that tells me that the state is picking up the bill," Dr. Aaron calculated.

"Meaning?" Reuben asked.

"Meaning, you have no valid right to complain about anything, do you?"

"Well..." Reuben began, but found himself at a loss for words.

"That was a rhetorical question, Mr. Peterson...meaning it doesn't require an answer."

"Wow," Reuben said, "You're a bit of an asshole, aren't you?"

"Interesting. How does that make you feel?" Dr. Aaron asked him, figuratively putting on his Freud hat.

The psychotherapist seemed less than helpful for the remainder of the session, as he generally just rephrased what Reuben told him, but repeated it back as a question. When they were out of time, Reuben was excused, and allowed to have some downtime before dinner. Patients weren't given lunch at this incompetent, unethical facility, which didn't bother Reuben in the slightest, as he decided to fast for the remainder of his sentence.

Reuben had nothing to look forward to. His stomach churned, and his flamboyant bunkmate was no positive distraction, so he decided to go against his better judgment and sit in on art therapy. This was held in an enclosed recreational area, where patients often walked in circles just to get exercise, since the patients were never authorized to venture outdoors, even for a transient period.

There were also tables off on the side, where patients either participated in art therapy, or entertained themselves with various toys. There was a *SIMON* electronic memory game, a *Raggedy Ann* doll, a complete set of *Charlie's Angels* dolls, and a set of walkie talkies. Art therapy was at least an activity that wasn't supervised, so that was appealing. Reuben was worried about being made to feel like a circus freak again, but would quickly learn that the patients who partook in this crafts diversion, were too tranquilized to notice. There were four people in total, including Reuben. He sat across from Bethany, at the white granite heavy-duty folding table. She was visibly heavily medicated, which explained how she was able to sit at the table, with others. Benjamin was there sitting beside her, of course, to make certain that she wasn't touched by anyone, and that people respected her feelings. Benjamin wasn't actively participating, but simply there for Bethany's comfort and support. Thomas was the other person involved in this activity.

"You guys mind if I join you for this?" Reuben inquired politely, as he pulled out the chair he intended to sit upon.

"Don't invade Bethany's personal space," Benjamin stated, making his terms and conditions absolutely concrete up front.

Reuben dangled his head in the beginning, but once he saw how disconsolate Bethany was, it put him inexplicably at ease. He figured that his presence was inconsequential, which made him more comfortable around the others. The small gathering at the table seemed to be sad, but somehow gentle. They were kind people, who had just given up, in more ways than one. As Reuben spent time with them, he got the depressing feeling that his wretched peers were melancholy, but also content, giving no indication of ever expecting to (or even wishing to) be released or discharged.

"You ever wonder," Reuben began, "why we're not permitted to keep a toothbrush in our rooms, or have sheets or blankets on our mattresses, but yet...they provide us with battery operated toys? What's to stop any of us from sucking on a battery?"

"Mind your potatoes," William said, as he walked by them, showing them the *Mr. Potato Head* that he had chosen to play with. "Mind your potatoes," William said again, as he pushed the toy in Reuben's face, just close enough to where it came inches away from his nose.

Reuben found himself outside of his comfort zone, as he was engaging in dialogue with these total strangers, which was a breakthrough in itself. It didn't take long for him to realize that the people who ran the joint were the ones who should be locked up, and the ones who were stuck there, were actually not as crazy as they were told they were.

These psychiatric inmates had been put down for so long, that they had just accepted that they were useless and dysfunctional. Reuben sensed that many of them were scared to return to society, as if they had grown dependent on the stability of the facility, even though it was the facility that was slowly killing them. He also had the vague suspicion that the sole purpose of this art therapy was to merely entertain the bored mental patients. Reuben had begun to sense that most of the patients were quiet and too consumed in their own afflictions and adversities to pay much attention to him, but when he let his guard down, and let them in, he discovered that they were more interesting than they appeared to be on the surface.

"I sure miss Barbara," Thomas said aloud, out of the blue.

"Who's Barbara?" Reuben asked, making an effort to show interest.

"She's a patient that used to do crafts with us, who is undergoing electroshock therapy now," Benjamin answered.

"Why? What happened?" Reuben asked, once again trying to be attentive and inquisitive, at least for the purpose of simulation.

"She tried to strangle Nurse Carl, when he pulled her away from art therapy to meet with her psychiatrist," Thomas replied.

"Most of the time, life in the ward is utterly predictable. You get used to their humdrum routine, which can be comforting in its own right. But sometimes the doctors like to fuck with your head, and will change your schedule on a dime, inevitably when you're in the middle of playing cards, talking to the other patients, sleeping, reading, or watching television," Benjamin contributed.

"Yeah, and Nurse Carl was the worst one she could have chosen to lash out at," Thomas added, completely clueless that Nurse Carl had attempted to pull her away, that day, for something else entirely.

"Yeah, he's a real grueler," William chimed in again, eavesdropping on their private conversation, while walking around their table, and now stopping behind Reuben's chair. "He deserved what Barbara gave him, but I don't think she realized the nightmare that he'd unleash on her, as a result," William said to Reuben, putting his hands on the back of his chair, gripping it tightly, as if expecting the chair to magically launch into space.

Thomas suddenly put his index finger up to his face, so that his knuckle was pressed up against his nostrils. His nose scrunched up, as if he were about to lose control of his sinuses. Reuben kept thinking Thomas would courteously turn around, or at least cover his mouth, but apparently Thomas wasn't concerned about spreading germs...he was just terrified of catching them.

"A-A-Ah choo!" Thomas let out, as he sneezed on the table in front of him, misting the others with his liquid mucus.

"Damn, Thomas," Benjamin said, "You sprayed flem everywhere. Cover your mouth next time, man."

"Oh man," Thomas said, as he started to panic, "This is it," he added, as he clearly began to get overwhelmed with a blizzard of anxiety.

"What's it?" Reuben asked.

"This is the beginning of the flu. I've got the flu. Or maybe it's something worse? Yeah, I bet it is. I bet I've got something worse. And my throat is hurting now, when I swallow. That's strep throat right there, at the very least."

"Maybe you just have a common cold? You ever consider that possibility?" Benjamin asked.

"No. I'm never that blessed. I'm susceptible to getting every scourge and syndrome under the sun," Thomas insisted. "God makes sure of that."

"You sure you're not self-diagnosing some of these ailments, you profess to get so frequently?" Benjamin asked.

"Yeah, he's a dick," Bethany said, who hadn't spoken at the table until now, offering a belated, delayed response to the comment made earlier about Nurse Carl being the bringer of Barbara's grief, and the primary source of her agony.

As they continued to utilize and play with their wicker box of crayons and their huge knitted bag of intricate stick-ons, glitter, foam shapes and rubber creatures, to make their childlike pictures, their creative collaboration was bluntly impeded by Nurse Gregory, who rolled in a metal, two-layered cart, stacked and packed with books. Everyone, but the small group at the table, immediately rushed over to search through the literary selection. Chad hurried over to ask Nurse Gregory, once again, if he could hook him up with some adult reading material.

"Okay," Nurse Gregory said, "You guys know the rules. Only one book per customer," he said, even though there was obviously no charge for checking out the used paperbacks, especially since they had to return what they took, the following week.

"Hey, Nurse Gregory," Chad said, casually, "Any chance of getting a righteous magazine from you today? Particularly either a *Hustler* or a *Penthouse*?"

"Look, Chad," Nurse Gregory said, "You know I try and be there for you guys, but I can only do what's within reason. If I brought material like that in this place, it would mean my job. I got a wife and a couple of ninos at home. I can't be irresponsible. I don't have that luxury of being reckless, or slacking off."

"Hey Chad," Kenneth called out, "What do you need those monthly periodicals for? Is something wrong with your mojo? Why don't you gather up all your phantoms and phantasms, that only you can see, and have a fake orgy with them in your room?" he said, mocking Chad's mental illness in front of the audience, "Since you can't snag any real pelt."

"Up your nose with a rubber hose, asshole! Not that it's any of your fucking business," the self-proclaimed Casanova said in his own defense, "but you don't know jack squat about anything! For your information, I happened to have lost a stellar bunny of mine years ago, who meant everything to me, and whom I miss more than words! So, though I don't need to explain myself to the likes of you, I don't find it very funny when you make fun of me when she comes to visit," he said, confirming that he does, in fact, see his deceased lover. "I'd appreciate if you wouldn't spew your defamatory insults about her as loud as you do, since she's sleeping in my bunk at this very moment, from the party hardy we did last night" Chad added, digging his own grave even deeper.

"You're so out to lunch, Chad," William said, "but we love you anyway," he said, patting the flustered Chad on the back of his shoulder blade.

"Phooey," Kenneth said back, "If you have a foxy lady in your room, she's either plastic or her name's Mary Jane."

"Get bent," Chad said, in response to Kenneth's continual ridicule.

The reading selection was fairly lame, mostly composed, and consisting of, cheesy romance novels and book three of a science-fiction series. There was a copy of the Holy Bible, which nobody seemed to want. There was also a copy of both the Book of Mormon and the Quran, which everyone passed by as well. Reuben found a copy of Alex Comfort's book, *The Joy of Sex*, and quickly grabbed it up, before the others noticed that it was even in the mix. There was a large stack of Alcoholics Anonymous and Narcotics Anonymous pamphlets. It was getting close to dinnertime, and Reuben grew restless for something, or anything, to make him forget the hunger that stalked him so acutely.

"You're not going to pick a book, for this week?" Reuben asked, directing his question at Thomas. "There's got to be one here, with some pictures in it,"

Reuben noted, not to wisecrack, but to just try and be helpful.

"Are you kidding?" Thomas clamored, "I can't remember when I had my last tetanus shot, and that rollaway cart is metal...and old metal at that. What if I accidentally brush my hand up against the rust spots, and break the skin?"

Thomas had upset himself so much, just thinking about hurting himself on the cart, and therefore exposing himself, and making himself more vulnerable, to the likelihood of more health problems, that he lost his balance, fell back on his chair, and hit the ground, simply due to his over excitement.

"No thanks," Thomas said, as he lay sprawled on the floor, on his back. "Great," he said, "Now I think I broke something."

Reuben excused himself from the art enthusiasts and wandered over to the dining section, where he witnessed the kitchen staff putting out little bowls of lime flavored *Jell-O* mold, with shredded carrots inside, and Cool Whip on top. He also saw them bring out paper plates topped with cardboard quality pizza, which was undoubtedly soaked in liquefied garlic. Shaking his head in foretold disillusion, he was about to return to his room, when he noticed that they had set out a silver coffee urn. It only dispensed decaf, and no creamer or sugar was offered as a condiment, but at least it was something he could consume that was safe.

They had also set out a soda fountain, offering five brands of pop, *RC Cola*, *TaB*, *Bubble Up*, Strawberry flavored *Rondo*, or Black Cherry *Donald Duck* soda, all of which had been watered down, to save money.

"Are you going to finish your plate this time?" Nurse Monica said with a smile, as she practically snuck up on him.

Reuben jumped slightly, as she startled him. "Um, actually, I'm contemplating on maybe skipping supper, like you suggested. The limited menu selection doesn't look any more appetizing for this meal," he replied, as he helped himself to a cup of black coffee, to carry back to his room. Nurse Monica noticed that he had *The Joy of Sex* tucked away under his arm, the whole time they were talking.

"You know," Nurse Monica said, "it would be much easier to pour that cup of Joe, if you just put down that book you're carrying," she said, with a smile on her face.

Reuben, embarrassed, pretended he didn't hear that, and began to walk away from her.

"If you need help with your studying," she said, "let me know. I can make a great tutor."

As Reuben walked back towards his room, he saw Joshua in the corner, kneeling down, holding a couple of *Lincoln Logs* in his hands. He was fervently rubbing them together, moving them faster and harder against each other, as if he was trying to somehow ignite a fire with the imitation wood. As Reuben walked passed him, trying not to make eye contact, Joshua briefly stopped what he was doing, just long enough to glance up at Reuben with a stare of hateful bias. Reuben wondered if maybe he had more in common with his disturbed roommate than he realized. Reuben wasn't queer, by any means, but he could relate to having sexual frustration...and understood how such bottled up, untended needs could result in such a display of anger or even lunacy. Perhaps they both needed to get laid?

Hours later, around three in the morning, Reuben laid wide-awake on the bottom bunk. His fabulously gay roommate is in the bed above him, resting like the dead.

Reuben had been busy fondling himself under his pants, to the arousing thoughts of the girl whom he felt to be the one he had unknowingly longed so long for. He hadn't been able to sleep, because he was no longer serene or satisfied with being unwanted and unloved. She had changed all that with just an accepting glance and a warm smile.

Though he didn't yet know her name, she had charmed his hardened heart, and he wanted her so intensely, that his passion for her temporarily made him forget that she was beyond his league and could never feasibly return his obsessive hunger.

Getting out of bed, he walks to his door, and slightly cracks it open, just enough to look down the dingy hallway. Though the hall was somber, Reuben had strong night vision, and could see that there was only one overnight nurse on watch, and she had fallen asleep on the job.

Keeping as quiet as he could muster, he slowly made his way to the girl's room, as he began to hear muffled moaning, which got clearer as he neared her coveted door.

Looking through the corner of her window, he sees her on her knees blowing a male nurse (one he hadn't officially met or been introduced to), who is sitting on the edge of her bed. The nurse was a buff, steroid-injected goon, and his hands are on the back of her head, pushing and guiding, while his eyes are shut.

Since the nurse's head is tilted backward to the ceiling, and her shagadelic head is preoccupied with what her mouth and throat are doing, Reuben's spectating isn't seen by either of them. Though it understandably upset Reuben that she was blowing someone who wasn't him, watching her in action drove him crazy.

OCTOBER 29, 1977

Reuben was awoken earlier this morning, to attend his first group therapy session. To his dismay, Dr. Aaron would be the one moderating these sessions. Before officially launching the session, Dr. Aaron started off by telling the group that they needed to believe in a Supreme Being in order to conquer and overcome their depression. He delivered this short sermon, as he was holding a copy of the Holy Bible on his lap, which looked like it had never been opened or read. This was irritating, not because any of the patients had any burning hatred for God, but because it was no secret that Dr. Aaron was no man of God.

"Okay," the smug hypocrite initiated, "Let's go around the room, and take turns speaking. If you don't want to talk, I won't push it. But, I'd like everyone to at least introduce themselves, as we have a new member joining us. It looks like we're all accounted for today, which is nice to see. Some of you have been skipping, which you know we object to, which doesn't help your rehabilitation or recovery. Why don't you set us off, Chad," he said to the patient on his left.

There were nine patients in attendance, and they all sat in cushioned, folding metal chairs...all except for

Kenneth, who was exclusively allowed to sit in a recliner, being as he was just too obese for the human-sized chairs. They were all arranged in a circle, with Dr. Aaron, one of the many head psychiatrists on staff, at the helm, to lead the session. As instructed, everyone would go around the room, taking turns sharing their stories. Most would simply keep it basic, announcing their first names, and briefly disclosing why they thought they were there. Most of them ranged from their mid-twenties to just older than Reuben. Reuben was expecting most of them to speak of disturbing, taboo fantasies about their mothers, or psychotic, haunted hallucinations of dead loved ones; or perhaps surprise revelations that some of them were chronic bed wetters, cheating sociopaths, survivors of alien abduction, pathological liars, or textbook multiple personality disorders. In any case, Reuben couldn't have begun to prepare for what would actually come to be.

"Well, my name is Chad. I'm...well, I'm not going to say my age. Age is just a number anyway. I'm here because I was arrested for streaking in public, and then laying naked in the *Wendy's* salad bar."

"And?" Dr. Aaron nudged Chad, prodding him to share more than he was willing, about what led him here.

"I'm told I have what's called schizoaffective disorder," Chad continued. "This means that I see what's not there, hear those who aren't there, and I also have a tendency to get paranoid, and confused in my speech and thought process," Chad elaborated.

"Thank you," Dr. Aaron said. "Very good. Okay, Benjamin, give us the skinny."

"I'm Benjamin. I used to be awkwardly shy. Still am, to a point, I guess. I've been told I'm anorexic, though I don't see that as being the case. And, I'm told that I have a lack of enthusiasm or eagerness for activity...a condition they like to call melancholia."

"Thank you..." Dr. Aaron started, trying to move on to the next patient.

"This is my hip friend, Bethany," Benjamin said, interrupting Dr. Aaron and speaking for Bethany, who was next in line to share. "She's very sweet, but very fragile. She doesn't like to be in crowded areas, or enclosed, uncontrolled spaces with a lot of people. She also doesn't like to be touched."

"As we can all see, Benja..." Dr. Aaron tried to interject again, only to yet again be cut off.

"Don't laugh at her," Benjamin continued, "It's not her fault. She suffers from Anthropophobia, which makes her scared of people."

Dr. Aaron waited a moment, to make sure that Benjamin was done, before proceeding.

"Thank you, Benjamin," Dr. Aaron said. "As we can all clearly see, Benjamin also has an overprotective personality."

"I'm Reuben Ian Peterson...or RIP for short. That's what my parents would call me. They came to this country from Germany, as you can probably gather from my accent. And, no, in case you're asking yourselves, I don't have any connection to the Nazi Movement."

Thomas blushed in embarrassment, as Kenneth gave him a guilt-trip look, as if to silently say *I told you so*.

"I know you all have also noticed that I look strange, unreal...even sick" Reuben continued, with his elbows resting on his knees, and his eyes facing the floor between his feet, which were spread apart. "Some have even said I look like a monster. Well, there's a reason for that, and to my regret, it's beyond my control. I was born with a blood disorder, that's very rare, and very detrimental to my health. It's called porphyria, and is what makes me look like this. That being said, I'm here because I tried to kill myself," Reuben shared, running one of his hands through his red, shoulder-length, straight hair. "I'm told I have PTSD...otherwise known as Post Traumatic Stress Disorder, which I owe thanks to both God and my parents for that."

"O-kay," Dr. Aaron said, as if not sure how to respond to that, "William, can you share with us?"

"I'm William. My name is William. I've been accused of being a *bible thumper*, which is offensive to me, because I would never dream of doing that to a

Bible, or any book, for that matter. I have what they call bibliomania. Apparently, I'm a huge fan of collecting...or what they call *hoarding*...too many books. Like that's some zappy crime."

"William doesn't simply collect books, but he collects so many that his wife left him, because there was no room in the house for her or her things. He also doesn't acquire them to read them, but just to stick on the shelf and gawk at," Dr. Aaron added. "That being said, I have a great deal of respect for William, as he may be sick, but he clearly loves the Lord," Dr. Aaron said, winking and smiling at William, to show his unwavering support.

"I also lost my job, because..." William began again.

"You lost your job?" Chad asked, attempting to be funny. "Did you look for it?"

Dr. Aaron just shook his head, holding his forehead as if to imply he was feeling a migraine coming on.

"Fine," William rephrased, "I got fired from my job, because of my disease. I had missed too much work, because of my alleged, so-called *obsessive-compulsive* attention to my collection."

"Thank you," Dr. Aaron said. "Thank you for sharing with us."

"My name is Thomas. I was diagnosed as being a neurotic hypochondriac."

"No shit," Kenneth remarked, with insolence.

"People think I think that the world is out to get me, and that I'm going to die from anything and everything," Thomas said, choosing to ignore Kenneth's brazen scorn.

"Thank you, Thomas," Dr. Aaron said, as he turned and looked at Kenneth, expecting more of the worst from him.

"I'll pass," Kenneth said, shrugging off his obligation to the pack.

"What's wrong, Ken?" Reuben asked. "You can dish it out, but when it comes to talking about yourself, you're a pansy?"

"Come over here, and say that to my face, string bean!" Kenneth exclaimed, referring to his skinny arms, offended and embarrassed that Reuben had the nerve to insult him in front of the group.

"I thought Joshua was the pansy?" Chad said, not realizing that Reuben referred to the *coward* definition, instead of the *sissy* meaning.

Joshua grinned in pride, as if complimented by the unintended homosexual label.

Reuben didn't react, but simply continued to look at Kenneth, showing him that he wasn't afraid of him, by not turning his eyes away.

"Come on, you freak! Come over here and say that again, and see where it gets ya!" Kenneth shouted again, not weakening his threat.

"Okay," Dr. Aaron intervened, "That's enough. Reuben, you shouldn't have said what you said. Kenneth, you don't want to be in a real prison tomorrow, do you?" the doctor asked him, speaking to both of them like they were little children.

Kenneth began to calm down, agreeing that he didn't want to be transferred to an actual maximum-security penitentiary. Kenneth was the one patient there, who was court ordered to be there. It was either there or prison, for him.

"That's better," Dr. Aaron said. "Now, Reuben, would you like to apologize to Kenneth?" he asked, still speaking to Reuben as if he were six-years-old.

"Not particularly," Reuben answered honestly. "I think he should share his story with the class. The rest of us did. I think it's only fair."

Dawn smiled at him, impressed with Reuben's display of courage, and with the way he had stood up for Thomas. Reuben picked up on her smile of approval, which only encouraged him more to show off for her.

Kenneth's heart rate began to accelerate again, and his high blood pressure began to escalate more so than before, as he looked at Reuben with a mean streak just waiting to erupt.

"Kenneth," Dr. Aaron said, "I must agree. Reuben is quite correct. It is your..."

"Actually, why don't I do it for him?" Reuben interrupted, "Hi, my name is Kenneth. I'm a hot tempered know-it-all who just doesn't know when to put that damned spoon and fork down."

"Don't forget bipolar," Benjamin contributed.

"Yeah, he's definitely polar," Chad agreed, "but the *bi* part remains to be seen," he said, laughing.

"Ooohhh, that was a major burn," Benjamin said, joining in on the joke, at Kenneth's expense.

"That's it!" Kenneth said, getting up out of his privileged recliner and running towards Reuben. The rest of the group just watched in utter awe, as Reuben amazed all of them by not getting up out of his chair to avoid a beat down. Instead, Reuben just sat there, calm and smiling, as if he was either the poster-boy for fearlessness or just simply welcoming death. Dr. Aaron blew on his whistle, which he had threaded on a lariat, that he kept around his neck and tucked securely under his overpriced, plaid dress shirt and long, white lab coat. Security couldn't arrive fast enough to stop Kenneth's oncoming stampede. Just as help came into the room, Kenneth pulverized Reuben, by ramming into him, with his goliath-sized body, causing Reuben to not only forcefully fall backwards, but be knocked clear across the room. Before Reuben could get up, or even collect his thoughts, Kenneth had straddled him, nearly crushing him with his elephant-like weight.

"Do you want a hertz donut?" Kenneth asked Reuben, while sitting on top of him.

"What?" Reuben asked, in an already confused state.

Kenneth put his fat hand underneath Reuben's shirt, and grabbed his right nipple, only to twist it with force.

"Hurts, don't it?" he said, laughing, amused with himself and his bullying ways.

Nurse Carl and Nurse Gregory came rushing over to Kenneth, and stuck him with a hypodermic needle, drugging him with a strong sedative, and giving him a dosage high enough to put a wild stallion to sleep. They quickly pulled him off of Reuben, who was now gasping for breath.

"What do you want us to do with him?" Nurse Carl asked Dr. Aaron, "I don't think he'll fit in a strait jacket."

"Just lock him up in the observatory room," the doctor ordered, "Let him cool off in solitary for the rest of the day."

After the male nurses had hauled Kenneth off, Dr. Aaron looked at Reuben with a stern look of disappointment.

"Mr. Peterson," he said, "That was not helpful. Nothing is ever solved by deliberately antagonizing a hot head like Kenneth. We all know he's a ticking time bomb. You're not helping matters any by egging him on."

"Reuben's cruisin' for a bruisin.' Reuben's cruisin' for a bruisin," Thomas said, in a somewhat delayed response to what had just taken place between Kenneth and Reuben.

"Copy," Reuben agreed with Dr. Aaron. "I'm sorry."

"That being said," Dr. Aaron continued, completely caught off guard, not anticipating that Reuben would admit he was wrong or apologize for it, "I will not tolerate violence in this ward. Hence, why I'm punishing Kenneth."

There were only two patients left who hadn't shared with the group. It was finally going to happen. Reuben was finally going to get to hear her story...the gorgeous, buxom, shapely, brunette bombshell that he couldn't get out of his already troubled mind. This is what Reuben had been anxiously awaiting. He would finally get to know about this owner of his passion. He was impatiently eager to not only unveil what category of mental illness she represented, but to learn as much detail about who she was, as possible.

"She's a brick house," Chad blurted out, referring to Dawn's intoxicating well-proportioned figure. "If Dawn made a poster of herself, like that Farrah Fawcett one I have hanging on my wall at home, I'd never leave my bedroom."

"Yes," Dr. Aaron agreed, "We all know that. Now, let her speak, Chad. It's her turn. You had your turn," again speaking to the live-in patients in a condescending tone of voice.

"If you had a poster of Dawn like that," William added, "You wouldn't need any *Scotch* tape to stick it to the wall," he muttered under his voice, just barely loud enough for everyone in the circle to hear.

"Now that's quite enough," Dr. Aaron sternly announced, as the rest of the group chuckled and snickered at William's comment. The only ones not laughing in amusement were of course, Chad, Dawn...and Reuben. "Please, Dawn," Dr. Aaron said, "Share your story with the group," he said in a consoling tone, "I promise there won't be any further interruptions," he added, as he gave the rest of the group a dirty look, as if to use his body language to warn them one final time.

"My name is Dawn Moon," she said in an almost mousy voice, "Much like Reuben, I also suffer from PTSD." Reuben saw that Dawn began to get nervous, as if afraid to share with the group, "Um, this is Joshua," she said, trying to take the focus off her, and move on to the last person. "Joshua doesn't talk. He's not mute, but he just chooses not to speak. He's a bit of a panty waste, but only because his bitch ex-wife screwed him over so badly, that she literally made him switch teams," she said, with a phony baloney, forced smile, making it clear that she suddenly wanted to be anywhere but there. "Now, he's a Nancy-Boy, but not one you want to turn your back on. Now, Joshua just takes out his anger by burning the possessions of his old flames, or trying to burn those who piss him off."

"Now, Dawn," Dr. Aaron said, again using the patronizing tone of his already condescending manner. "Relax. Just relax. It's okay. We all love you here, don't we?" he said, asking the group for moral support on her behalf.

"Yeah," the group said simultaneously and collectively, not excluding her ginger-headed secret admirer.

"By the way," Dr. Aaron said, "Before we let Dawn begin again, and tell us the truth about herself, I just wanted to clarify that Joshua is not only here for being a pyromaniac, but that he was traumatized when he was a young boy. From what I read in his file, his father had ran a bath for him, not paying attention to the water temperature. When he put Joshua in the bathtub, the water was so hot that it scolded him. What made it worse was, he never cried out or communicated this to his father...because he liked it. He enjoyed the pain. He thrived on it. When the father finally realized what he had accidentally done, he screamed for help, and quickly lifted Joshua out of the tub. His wife called for an ambulance, and Joshua was treated that night for second and third degree burns.

His father never forgave himself, and became an alcoholic. His mother eventually left and began a new family with another man. Joshua, because of the nerve damage that resulted from that experience, not only became fond of burning things, but became immune to physical pain...and even found he enjoys giving and receiving fire. Okay, Dawn, we're ready."

"My name is Dawn," she began again, closing her legs and tightening her inner thighs around her folded hands, which were pressed up against her warm vaginal region, as she leaned forward. "I'm eighteen. I arrived here almost a year ago, shortly before I was to start my senior year of High School. I came here involuntarily. My preacher father came upstairs, when he noticed water leaking from the ceiling, and found me incoherent in the overflowing bathtub, after downing a handful of sleeping pills. I was trying to escape from having to go to court for aggravated assault," she said as she covered her mouth to cough. "I was very resistant the first day or two here, but I was assigned a great psychiatrist, who told me that pills don't listen to me, love me, or give me encouragement. Eventually, I came around, and got along socially with the other patients and staff."

"That was very nice," Dr. Aaron complimented, "Very nice indeed. I'm Dr. Aaron. I went to school for a long time, to be where I am today. I don't have any issues or problems, and because of my superior intellect and prestigious education, I can do what I love, and be here for misfortunate misfits like yourselves."

Reuben noticed the way Dr. Aaron was ogling Dawn, as he vocally approved what she had to say, and likely relished even more what she chose to not say. Dawn was convincing, to the point where she could have easily won a best actress award. Reuben guessed that she had memorized this speech, beforehand, as if to prevent herself from mistakenly exposing her real feelings, or letting something slip that she preferred to keep secret and hidden. Reuben had seen enough to know that there was much more to her concealed tale, and figured that it must be darker than he could have ever possibly imagined or fathomed on his own.

"I can dig that," Reuben blurted out, even though his turn had already came and passed. "If you were more like me, you wouldn't have required sleeping aids. I used to sleep all day, and sometimes through the night as well. I found it helped pass the time, and kept me from dwelling on my loneliness and solitude. It also helped me see my folks as seldom as possible, if I just slept my life away in the cellar. I once bought into the God thing. I was raised to. But my parents reamed me, both verbally and physically, and kept me tucked away in the basement. They told me it was for my own good, as I do have a bona fide malady, which puts me in peril around sunlight, but it was because they were mortified of me. I was an embarrassment, an abomination unto the Almighty, as they reminded me of that often. They were devout Catholics, and even volunteered regularly at their church."

As Reuben listened to himself speak about his parents, he perceived that he was doing so in the past tense. Considering that his parents were still alive, this was highly inapt. Reuben subconsciously analyzed that perhaps he referred to them as historical, since he knew they were glad to be rid of him and because somehow he knew, deep in his lost soul, that he wouldn't be seeing them again.

"It behooves me to tell you that your mother brought you here, to get you help, Mr. Peterson," Dr. Aaron interjected what Reuben had said, reiterating what he had told him before, in the confidence and privacy of his office.

"Yeah, and we all know how helpful you and your madhouse are, don't we, doctor?" Reuben added, in his defense. "She probably brought me here, to evade interrogation, if the pigs found me dead in her house."

Dawn suddenly recognized Reuben as the man who was spying on her, and who had saved her from falling, while she was on the phone with one of her booty calls back home.

"Okay, that will be quite enough," the controlling doctor said, not advocating where he saw this heated discourse going.

"We have that in common," Dawn added, "I was molested by my father, who is an orthodox minister," she said, suddenly feeling comfortable with the idea of opening up more...at least to Reuben, anyway. She caught herself directing her undivided concentration on Reuben, as if wearing invisible blinders that mentally blocked everyone else out from her line of view.

"I'm sorry," Reuben apologized, "I d-d-didn't intend to stir up b-bad memories. Forgive me," Reuben stuttered, not because of what he had said, but whom he had said it to.

"What makes parents do this to their kids?" Dawn asked Reuben, as if the other people in the circle had literally vanished, as she continued to engage in an exclusive one-on-one interview with Reuben.

The group could almost see the steam coming out of Dr. Aaron's ears, as he grew irate, watching their discussion somehow evolve into a personal exchange between Reuben and Dawn. Dr. Aaron had lost control, and that fueled a furious rage that only he knew existed.

"Your parents love you!" Dr. Aaron exclaimed, trying direly to regain the steering wheel of the session, "Again, why would they have brought you here, if they didn't care?"

"It's simple," Reuben began, "I should have seen it before. They must have calculated that if we were legally labeled as crazy, it would free them of all accountability for their sins against us."

"That's crazy," the ostensible doctor declared.

"Is it?" Reuben asked, "Who believes a mental patient? Think about it. By having us marked as insane, and inserting us into this bedlam, it eludes them of all legal responsibility or any psychological guilt."

"Okay," Dr. Aaron said, "I think that's good for today. Let's cut this short, and rejoin tomorrow. Hopefully with a better attitude," the putative doctor added, as he threw his tattered Bible down on the floor in front of him, and slapped his knees with his palms, before getting up from his sanctimonious seat.

William immediately rose up from his chair and went over to where the Bible laid, and quickly scooped it off the dirty floor.

"I can't believe Dr. Aaron did that," William said, "That's not the way you treat sacred books," he added, as he inconspicuously shoved the Bible down his pants, as if making a futile attempt to somehow shoplift it from the mental ward.

As the group casually dispersed and the individual patients went their separate ways, staying within the confines of the sanitarium, Bethany and Benjamin stopped dead in their tracks.

"Oh my God," Chad said, "It's Barbara."

"Oh my God," Benjamin said, "I'm so buggin' out right now."

"She looks so Zen," Thomas added, with a despondent look on his face.

The four of them stood frozen in incredulity, as their stolen friend, who had been absent for a lengthy period of time, applied what limited energy she had left to trudge into the conference room. Barbara looked as if she had been thoroughly lobotomized, as she moved like a mindless zombie who had long suffered from chronic insomnia. Reuben, who was once again following Dawn like a dependent puppy, broke from his mission of hedonistic debauchery, and selflessly hastened over to Barbara. His clinical peers just stood in utter shock, as Reuben quickly motioned to help place the catatonic woman in a cushioned metal chair. Bethany, Chad, and Benjamin trailed almost obediently behind him, as did the human sugar to Reuben's sweet tooth. Dawn had been making her way out the door, when she descried Reuben's compassionate gesture, and was so taken by his genuine kindness and empathy that she hung her mouth open and panted. Reuben knelt humbly before Barbara, with torrid tears in his organically bloodshot eyes, as the stunning Dawn laid her solicitous hand on his gelid shoulder.

"That's not quite what I'd call it," Reuben said, in response to Thomas's keen yet misinterpreted observation. "This woman's not at peace, Thomas. She's had pieces taken out of her."

"You're not jive talking," Chad said, agreeing with Reuben that Barbara had been severely damaged and tampered with.

"Come on," Dawn gently urged Reuben, "They'll keep her company. Come on, 'Red'…let's book."

"Book?" William asked, instantly excited at the mere sound of his favorite word, "Where?"

Reuben picked himself up, and slowly but surely followed Dawn out of the banquet-sized area.

"Check you later, Dawn," Chad said, as he watched her totally hot ass strut out of the room, significantly disappointed to see her arm-in-arm with Reuben. "One of these days," Chad said aloud to himself, "That stone cold fox will be mine."

"I wouldn't mind seeing her in a pair of hot pants," Thomas added.

"Fuck that," Chad said. "If she were mine, she'd never wear pants. Girls who come to my pad, aren't allowed to wear any clothes…at least not from the waist down…unless they're edible pants or sweat pants, that give me easy access and are easy to take off."

"That's harsh," William said, coming up behind them, after overhearing their brief but overheated conversation, "Dawn's a human being, not a piece of meat."

"Right on, spaz" Chad said, "that fine, foxy mama is primo grade stash, and I'm dying to toke it…over and over and over again...till that flame is tamed, and branded with my name," Chad added with drool practically dripping from the corner of his cotton mouth.

While the immediately flirtatious couple made their way to the main hallway, William hustled to catch up with them, and cut them off, to grab their attention for a moment.

"Hey, Reuben, wait up, man!" William said, "I just wanted to say that I think it was really admirable what you did back there for Thomas, man. That Kenneth is always ragging on those of us who are smaller and weaker than him, which pretty much includes all of us. You're alright, man," William said, as he extended his hand for Reuben to take and shake.

"No problem," Reuben said, as he courteously and politely shook William's offered yet self-righteous hand. "Don't let Kenneth get to you, man. He's just a jive turkey. His bark is much worse than his bite. I guarantee it."

Reuben, because of his parents' neglect and abuse, had been isolated and secluded all of his life, and was therefore a social virgin. That being said, it was in his instinctive DNA, to have a natural sixth sense about people. He found he had a God-given knack for identifying and recognizing a person's true character...or lack thereof.

Kenneth, however, wasn't one of those subjects that were difficult to read, as there were no hidden layers to his individuality. Kenneth was one of those few callous sadists that made no effort to hide it or cover it up, for selfish gain or blissful pleasure. Where others were easily manipulated and deceived, Reuben was quick to see through people's seductive facade. This was partly what drew him to Dawn, aside from his intense attraction and obsessive infatuation to her phenomenal and incomparable beauty. He saw in her, an impaired but authentic heart, and one with wounds but without agenda. This led him to having a burning desire to learn more about who she was and how she could fit into his palm and lap.

"Right on, man," William said, as he casually walked off, leaving Dawn and Reuben to resume their quality alone time.

Dawn led Reuben on a somewhat intimate detour to the smoking section, which she found to be more neutrally private. Taking the initiative in making the first move, she took Reuben by the hand. She sat on the lime green bench, and then eagerly ushered Reuben to sit close beside her.

"I really like your name?" Dawn said, consciously trying to break the ice further, earnestly anxious to learn as much as she can about this tall, dark, and mysterious man.

"Thanks," Reuben cordially responded, returning the genial smile he had received from her earlier. "I dig your name too."

Dawn gazed into Reuben's weary eyes, and saw that look she had become all too familiar with. She could tell when men craved her, and she saw this same look in him. This spooked her, but also intrigued her, as he also looked at her with undisputed warmth, which she wasn't at all familiar with or accustomed to.

"This place is so fucked," Dawn told him, "Fucked up the ass."

"So," Reuben began to respond, "Tell me what you're really thinking," he said sarcastically, to try and lighten up her mood a bit, with an inch of humor.

Dawn just gave him a dirty look, as if to silently warn him of what could be unleashed, if pushed hard enough to the edge.

"I know," Reuben said, in attempt to revert back to before his last comment, "I haven't been here as long as you have, but it's crystal clear to me that this lunatic institution is redefining the term, *malpractice*."

"They tell you that their primary concern is rehabilitating, deprogramming, and that their ultimate goal is to stabilize you," Dawn said, "but whatever they did to poor Barbara in there…is an entirely different story. It's fucking unforgivable."

Reuben wraps his gangly arms around her delicate neck, sensing that she's about to completely break down emotionally. His sensitive intuition proved to be both nurturing and reliable, as she began sobbing hysterically in his shoulder, as soon as he proffered it.

"They're supposed to give you medication, therapy, and wait for you to get saner...not turn you into a lifeless vegetable," Dawn said, sniveling into his uniform shirt and burying her pretty face in his constricted yet welcoming chest as he held her as close as he possibly could.

"I've noticed that the ward's policies are highly inconsistent, and very contradictory. They deprive us of, and deny us, certain amenities and luxuries, yet provide us with others that can equally be manipulated or manifested into suicidal weapons," Reuben verbally expressed, sufficiently impressing Dawn with his extensive use of vocabulary.

Dawn gleefully showed him her adorable dimples again, looking up at him as if he had been heaven sent. "Would you like to kiss me?" she hopefully invited, still snuggled tight in Reuben's foreign but protective arms.

Before Reuben could begin to answer her, Nurse Carl rudely imposed, popping in abruptly.

"Okay, you two," he said in a curt tone, "Let's go. Get back to your own rooms. Now...before I decide to report both of you," Carl threatened.

"Report us?" Reuben questioned, "For what exactly?" he asked boldly.

"Public display of affection," Nurse Carl answered. "That's not tolerated in this facility," he hypocritically addressed. Carl, of course, didn't mind PDA at all, just as long as he was engaged as a participant.

Reuben had finally met her, and was surprised and pleased to find her not repulsed by him. He was puzzled as to how she could be so affable, and not be chock full of rage, considering the tumult and tragedy that she had somehow survived. He was dumbfounded to learn that she was so young, or maybe he was just discovering that he had a fetish for the nubile. Maybe she didn't seem more mature than her age. Maybe he was just a perverted deviant. Though Dawn was part Caucasian, he could see the dominant percentage of Cherokee in her genes. Up until now, he had pondered the idea of escaping, but that had all changed. He now had a reason to want to be there. It plagued him that Dawn was whoring around with the staff, but he had it in his head that she would be his, even if he had to die to win her devoted affections.

Later that night, while the bland, humdrum voice over the PA system was alerting the sanatorium unit of the 15-minute last call before lights out, Reuben audaciously peeks again through Dawn's little window, only to get mooned by her in anger, as she yanks down her uniform pants and women's boy-brief underwear, to exhibit her exquisitely splendid, teenage ass.

This was one of Dawn's special privileges, as the rest of the patients were given cheap, thin, standard-issue underwear from the bughouse facility. Dawn had evidently been allowed to keep the underwear she brought with her, as they were pastel purple, with a white elastic waistband and pastel pink trim. They were form fitting, and obviously made of a cotton/spandex blend.

"Dang, so that's what the crack of Dawn looks like," he says aloud, but quietly to himself, as careful not to let her hear through the thick door.

Dawn had a tramp-stamp tattoo of a tribal wolf paw, just above her butt crack. He sees that she's patently and indubitably on her period, as there is a self-adhesive menstrual pad in her underwear that is marinated in blood.

"Come inside and eat me out," she says just loud enough for the person outside her door to hear, "I dare you."

She does this, presuming that it's one of the usual male RNs coming for more oppressive indulgence, not bothering to look to see who the spy is who is actually peeping in on her. As she bares her magnificent and flawless backside, she sticks out her middle finger, showing her lack of appreciation for their abusive mistreatment and brutal malpractice.

Though this would have effectively pushed most rational men away, seeing her in this natural state only turned Reuben on more. He even caught himself playing with himself, as he had subconsciously slid his wandering right hand down the front of his pants and touched himself to the embodiment of his lustful desires. It didn't even occur to him right then, that someone could be watching him or that he could get into trouble for his degenerate behavior. His tender heart and his aroused shaft wanted what they wanted, despite any reason or sensibility.

OCTOBER 30, 1977

Reuben was once again awoken fairly early, after another fidgety night of fondling himself to the whole idea of Dawn, whom he wondered might just be a cruel mirage. He was once again given his vague, anonymous pill, with his overtly noxious breakfast, which he only shammed and again refused to consume. As he watched his fellow inmates simultaneously devour their plates of edible garbage, Reuben became well aware that they were no longer staring in his general or immediate direction. Though this pleased him greatly, the afflicting stress being brought on by the monsters that governed the disreputable facility, was beginning to have an unnerving effect on him. Reuben caught himself nervously picking at his face, with his unnerving serrated fingers, and blinking frequently and heavily, as if desperately trying to constantly purge them from some annoying optical obstacle. About an hour after breakfast ended, he was given a mandatory order to report promptly to the nurse's station, to have his blood pressure and other vitals taken. Soon after this was achieved, it was group therapy time again. Kenneth was, of course, absent for this particular session.

"I really want to bang *Power Girl*," Chad said, sharing and revealing way too much personal information, as typically usual.

"Who's this *Power Girl* you speak of?" Dr. Aaron asked.

"Ummm...she's sort of an icon of pop culture. Duh." William responded, as he also hoarded comic books, along with all the myriad of other books he compulsively collected.

"Actually, she's quite honestly just a lame character in a pretty fruity comic book, that came out a couple of years ago." Thomas contributed. "The only thing substantially likable about her is the way she looks, and the fact that she has huge boobs."

Chad began to methodically play with himself, over his insipidly static pants.

"Chad!" Dr. Aaron said, suddenly noticing what Chad was doing, "Quit that."

"Aren't you afraid you'll get ink-poisoning?" Reuben asked Chad, making the others laugh and chuckle under their breath.

"Okay, that's quite enough of that," Dr. Aaron declared. "Let's not have a dreaded rerun of yesterday's grotesque display of total anarchy. I don't want to see any more outbursts. I just cannot allow anymore disturbances or disruptions."

This time, instead of taking turns going around the room, they were forced to sit and listen to the psychiatrist going on and on about job interviewing and other such things, none of which had anything to do with why they were there, or what had led them to being who they were or why they turned out how they did. Reuben slowly shook his head in frustration, at this vastly non-constructive topic.

"How is this relevant here?" Reuben queried.

"What do you mean, Mr. Peterson?" Dr. Aaron asked, visibly sighing, and growing impatient and intolerant with his proneness for contempt.

"No one will ever hire any of us, when we get out, so what's the point of going over helpful techniques for successful interviews?" Reuben proposed a legitimate question, making a strong case and valid argument.

"That's really a pathetic attitude. Think negative, and that's precisely what you'll get." Dr. Aaron arrogantly professed.

"No. I just know enough about how this country works. America doesn't hand out second chances, and neither does God. Once you get a blemish of any kind on your record, regardless of how petty or trivial, it haunts you forever, be it a misdemeanor, a felony, an unfounded allegation, a wrongful termination, or a stay at a loony bin" Reuben testified.

Reuben had very little life experience, if any at all, but he had spent an enormous amount of time reading the newspaper and flipping through diverse magazines, which his parents often provided him, to entertain him down in the damp basement. Various papers and periodicals were even often used and served as incentives or rewards, to motivate him to be on his best behavior and do exactly what he was told. Reuben knew about the world, just not so much from his own encounters. Other than his grim dealings with his parents, his personal education was slim to nil.

"Getting support here is all fine and dandy, but those of us who eventually get released from here, will inevitably have to face the dark reality again, of what it's like to be a citizen of this nation," Thomas said, in full agreement with Reuben's depressing yet factual outlook. "Once a person is labeled as being certifiable, their life is more or less over."

"Yeah, Chad" Bethany blurted out of the blue, "Aren't you afraid of getting ink poisoning?" she asked, arriving late to the game in her response to the previous conversation about *Power Girl*. "Why don't you fantasize about a real woman?"

"I don't want to peel out," William stated nervously, "I've been here for too long. The very thought of going out there...just terrifies me now."

William helped put the scattered puzzle pieces back into proper perspective for Reuben, as his words backed up what Reuben had spoken, thereby both confirming and representing the macabre reality of the asylum prepping the susceptible patients to be permanently disconnected from the outside world, who were already under the preconception that they are unwanted and unaccepted. These patients were vulnerable and somewhat impotent, and though most of them were horrified to come here, the concept of being discharged served as an even greater nightmare. Despite Reuben's social phobia, he was exceptionally and notably proud to see the others take a firm stand, and not cowardly hold their tongues in fear of being wrongfully judged or unfairly penalized. Though being in this psychiatric ward was slowly killing him in certain ways, it had also taught him that he isn't alone after all.

"I can tell, from listening to your opinionated views and convictions, that some of you have been severely burned by our judicial laws and governing authorities. That being said, however, this is neither the time nor the place to vent or dispute these tribulations. You people are making it very difficult to impossible, for me to effectively and efficiently conduct these sessions." the annoyed Dr. Aaron proceeded to elaborate in aggravated frustration.

"How does that make you feel?" Reuben asked sarcastically but courageously, turning the tables on the wicked doctor, and putting his figurative shoe on the aspired dictator's foot.

Though Reuben had once again made Dr. Aaron's job a tough challenge, by making a public spectacle of himself, the group session somehow returned to the premeditated lesson plan of job hunting. Reuben's apparent ambition of being an official nuisance had subsided, as if it had been nothing more than simply a moody phase.

The rest of the day passed slower than a busted lava lamp, while Reuben had begun to feel as if he had been there for nothing short of an eternity. It was soon that closing time again, to retire to their respective rooms, and visit their personalized dreamlands. Reuben compulsively risked peering in Dawn's spellbound window again, this time to be surprised off guard with finding the bombshell of his life. Dawn was expecting him this time, and had patiently waited by the door, quickly opening it and vigorously pulling him inside. Dawn was much stronger than she looked, and threw Reuben so aggressively across the white room, that it knocked him completely unconscious, when he collided his red head with her white wall.

Later, Reuben came to and regained his surroundings, finding himself on Dawn's bed. She was kneeling on the floor, at his side, stroking and caressing his sideburns and his crimson-colored widow's peak. Fortunately, Dawn was the one resident patient in the nuthouse who had her own room, where there were no intrusions…well, at least not from the other patients anyway. She had also been granted a softer queen-sized bed, as opposed to the standard twin-size that the other unluckier inmates were left to settle for.

"I'm so sorry" she apologized to him with watery eyes, "I thought you were one of them."

"N-n-n-no," Reuben stuttered anxiously, "I'm s-s-sorry. I s-s-shouldn't have been s-s-spying on you."

"Why were you?" Dawn asked him out of phony curiosity, now smiling seductively out of the corner of her enticing mouth.

"You're b-b-beautiful, and I wanted to just be n-near you. I know that must s-s-sound crazy."

"No," she said, "Not at all."

Dawn felt a hard lump on the back of his troubled head, as she continued to gently massage his scalp, running her soft fingers through his thick head of gritty red hair.

"I'm so sorry that I hurt you" she apologized again, while her eyes continued to tear up and now release liquid emotions down her smooth cheeks, "Please allow me to make it up to you."

Though Reuben was equally sheepish and stimulated about what was currently happening to him, he watched in blissful disbelief, as she unhurriedly pulled his pants down, just far enough to disrobe and expose his limp but excited penis. Then, before he could fully process the blessed miracle before him, he watched his fantasy commence, as she converted his pipe dream into a joyful reality, by submissively leaning over and placing her soft, wet mouth around his now growing erection. He was only average size, but was afflicted with an insatiable appetite that he was only now permitted to entertain; courtesy of the generous charity of his juvenile fixation. As her pretty head courteously bobbed up and down, not in sympathetic obligation but with altruistic enthusiasm, Reuben was torn between the euphoric sensation of pure newfound ecstasy, and the risk of being caught by one of the passing intrusive nurses. She fiercely jacked him off, while she attentively played with his hairy balls with her other hand, all while sucking his undefiled dick. Leaning his dazed head back, he soon temporarily forgot about the dicey jeopardy, and centralized his full attention on the hedonistic delight and overdue gratification.

As Reuben's throbbing manhood grew impressively stiffer in her welcoming mouth, he felt an unforeseen, irrepressible hankering come over him, and without warning, assumed unadulterated, overwhelming power. Reuben, though an inexperienced virgin, decisively took the reins of this rare opportunity, and seized Dawn by her long brunette hair, not to push her head further down his aroused shaft, but to pull her head off him entirely.

"What's wrong?" she asked, worried that she had unintentionally disappointed him somehow.

"Nothing, beautiful" he reassured her. "Nothing at all," he said without stuttering or stammering.

Reuben quickly sat up, and jumped off the bed as if he was running off of natural adrenaline, and dead set on having his way with her. Before Dawn knew what was happening, he had procured total command of her. He scooped her off the floor, as if she was a lightweight, and threw her aggressively, but gently, on the bed. Now it was his turn to ravage Dawn, and hopefully ruin her for other men in the process, as he vigorously pulled her pants completely off, and flung them carelessly on the floor. Dawn was petrified in embarrassment, but something magical kept her from fighting him off. He frightened her a little, but she also felt strangely connected to him. Though she didn't know him, she sensed that she belonged to him, like she was born to be in his arms. She felt ashamed of her body, wishing that she could have been sexier for him. Her vagina was abnormally bushy, and the pubic hair extended up to and around her naval. The curly hairs even spread about six inches down her inner thighs.

"Yeah" he said in a breathless sigh, "This isn't going to work this way."

This was his first time attempting intercourse, or engaging in any form of sexual activity with a partner. He needed easier access to her envied love canal. Without hesitation, Reuben flipped her over, so that she was lying flat on her stomach, forcing her to bear her firm, teenage buttocks to him. Her tush couldn't have been more flawless or scrumptious. Fortunately, unlike her frontal region, her luscious ass was hairless, and couldn't have been any smoother.

"Wow," he said.

"What's wrong?" she asked, worried that he was either disappointed or disgusted.

"Your ass is so beyond decent," he told her, astonished and amazed at how much more breathtakingly beautiful it was close up.

"Usually, they say a girl is indecent, when she's in this position with a guy," she said smiling, relieved that he wasn't let down by her abnormally hairy body.

"Well," he responded, "I'm not they."

Using his animal instinct, and his four lustful decades of waiting for a taste of indulgence, he kicked off the scrub-like pants that were still hugging his ankles, and pounced on her like a lion to its prey. Within a matter of seconds, he had pushed himself inside of her, from behind.

For the first time in his life, Reuben had found reason to take charge of his life, and motivation to go after what he wanted. Though his unhealthy obsession with Dawn had much to do with the way she looked, his insatiable hunger for her wasn't dirty or without meaning. His heart was just as involved and invested in his pursuit of her, as his forlorn penis was.

"Gimme some skin, baby" Reuben dominantly ordered her, as he thoroughly and euphorically enjoyed the way her overheated, moistened, miraculously tight hole felt on his rock hard phallus, which stood at attention exclusively for her.

Dawn came dangerous close to nearly blowing their cover, by letting out a pleasurable scream, but luckily Reuben caught her just in time, placing his coarse and perspiring palm around her hot mouth, to keep her muffled and discreet. It wasn't that Reuben was too big, but he unknowingly misdirected and penetrated the wrong hole.

Though Reuben was just less than six inches, he was impressively thick and she had never been sodomized before. Reuben moved his feet underneath hers, signaling to her to lock her feet around his, giving him the organic equivalent of restraining her ankles with metal cuffs. This kept her from squirming too much, by having her ankles entangled with his. As he mercilessly pounded her wet, snug orifice, Dawn twisted and twitched in painful discomfort, but once again was hesitant and reluctant to protest. Though it hurt, she also learned something new and insightful about herself; she got off on being dominated...at least by him. She actually began to kiss and lick Reuben's sweaty palm, which still firmly and steadily covered her open mouth, which turned Reuben on even further. She still writhed a bit, so Reuben laid down the law.

"Stop moving" he demanded, in a whispering but commanding voice, "You're going to push me out."

Reuben reached down with his free hand, and spread open her butt cheek, pulling it to the side as far as he could, allowing him to go deeper in her ass. Though his endowment may not have been as long as other men, he was still able to bump up against her cervix, as he thrust aggressively inside of her as if afraid that he would never again get another opportunity.

"Stop clenching your butt cheeks," he insisted, "Just relax. Let me have complete control."

Once again, she did as she was told, forcing herself to stay loose and obey without question, to allow him to go as deep as he could, in her forbidden canal. The fact that he was making love to her butt hole still managed to dodge him, leaving him with a disillusioned feeling of what it's like to fuck a pussy. He had also conveniently forgotten the night before, when he saw her on her period, which should have been a crystal indication to him now, that he was invading the wrong pleasure tunnel. She was wet with natural lubricant, but definitely not filled with a bloody substance that came to visit once a month.

"You're so tight," he complimented her on her anal cavity, struggling himself not to make too much noise, or draw too much attention, as he experienced sheer euphoria by penetrating and violating her anus.

"Feel the funk, Daddy," she replied, as she breathed heavily and moaned softly, as she began to feel the pain turn to pleasure, as he took his time exploring and stimulating her dark yet delicate erogenous zone.

Reuben was in pure heaven, as he never could have envisioned that lovemaking would be this exhilaratingly blissful. He decided then that he didn't want this to just be an illicit affair, but a lifetime of committed debauchery with her. He began to feel a filling sensation in his shaft, and soon felt an intense pressure at the head of his prick. Reuben had never even masturbated, at least not to completion, so he was entirely unprepared and naive on what to do or where to go. The pressure at the tip of his penis was so powerful, that it caused him agonizing pain. Dawn could feel that Reuben was ready to peak, and pleaded with him to let it go.

"It's okay," she said in her muzzled yet coherent voice, "You're my juicer, baby. Just let it go. Explode inside me."

"I don't know how," the ashamed Reuben answered in an awkward tone, as the pressure built up so mercilessly, that it literally brought him physical anguish to hold it all in.

Dawn suddenly realized that she was Reuben's first, and that he was uneducated and inexperienced in the ways of sex, though she couldn't tell by his astonishing stamina and incredible performance.

"That feeling you're feeling is cum. It wants to be released. Just let it go."

"How?" he asked her, once again embarrassed that he was so naive and ignorant.

"Relax your penis, and let it flow out of you…like you're peeing" she suggested, doing what she could to help the man of her dreams.

Reuben appreciated Dawn trying to be there for him, but didn't want to scare her off by urinating inside of her.

"It's okay" she said, immediately sensing that he was misinterpreting what she had just told him. "You won't pee in me. A penis can't pee and cum at the same time. Trust me, just let it out. Let it go. I felt your penis fill up. It's throbbing, because it needs to release your sperm. Set it free."

With that said, Reuben accepted her munificent invite of hospitality, and burst inside of her confined brown-eye. As he unloaded inside of her voluptuous bum, Reuben felt an exhilarating and overwhelming rush of adrenaline, as his liberating orgasm was more powerful and phenomenal than he ever could have imagined or requested.

Feeling this extremely potent, long overdue release inside of her cozy anal lair, it suddenly and unexpectedly brought Dawn to mind-blowing climax as well. This caught her completely off guard, as she had never experienced ecstasy this strong, nor had she ever been able to reach orgasm without somehow directly stimulating or kindling her vagina. Reuben still firmly cupped her mouth in his clammy palm, which was wise, considering the audibly unrestrained moaning that Dawn was now releasing. Reuben could feel her ardent climax, while he remained buried in her ass, as her vagina pulsated so fervently and intensely, that the vibrations were felt through the thin layer of skin that separated her two flesh-condoms. Reuben felt her ass clench and release, as she finished climaxing, making sure that every last drop of his cum inhabited her asshole as he continued to slowly grind up against her majestic rear end. As Reuben's erection gradually subsided, and he quickly grew soft and limp inside of her, he slowly pulled out, trying desperately to relish and savor each and every second that he was allowed to be inside of her. He had came so much and so prolifically, that as he ejected himself from her filled anus, he saw his thick, white jism ooze and leak out of her overstuffed asshole, as she had to fart some of it out. Dawn could feel it spill out of her ass, glaze her taint, and run down her leg.

"Gee whiz, Reuben," she said exhausted and nearly breathless, "Slam dunk, baby. You really gave me a butt load."

"I just fucked you in your ass," he said, just now realizing that he had been in her butt hole for the duration of their hot n' heavy intimate encounter, watching his beastly seed now spill in loads, from her young, tight anus.

"Yes you did," she responded, confirming without complaint.

Reuben, tired and drained, collapsed beside her.

"You have quite the libido" she complimented him, awestruck by his performance and endurance. "Not bad for an old man...not bad at all" she reaffirmed to him, while grinning from ear to ear. She struggled not to smile, as to not give him an ego, but the more she tried, the harder it was not to.

"You make it sound like I just competed in the *Geriatric Olympics*" he said back to her. "I don't need a heart monitor just yet," he added, still lying next to her.

Dawn curled up against Reuben, and laid the side of her head on his bare chest, as he threw his arm around her, as if to try to pull her in even closer. "Oh, I beg to differ" she argued, as she listened to, and felt, his heart race a mile a minute, as if it were close to busting out and breaking free...not that he wished to be free from her...as it was quite the opposite.

As Reuben gasped for breath and gripped his tight chest, she used what little energy she had left to push her upper body up, with both of her arms, which were now trembling at the elbows. Dawn noticed that Reuben's flaccid dick was still seeping sperm.

"You're still cumming," she said, as they both watched it trickle over his ginger-spiced nuts, which had a minimal amount of curly hairs on them.

"Stick it in your mouth," he begged desperately but dominantly, "Please, Dawn. I want you to drink from me."

Though most girls would have felt degraded and offended by this bold and naughty request, Dawn's sole reason for feeling uncomfortable with the idea of tasting his cock, was only because it had just been in her ass. Putting her awkwardness and inhibitions aside, she obediently submitted to his wishes, and followed his instructions without question or dispute. Dawn had been conditioned to obey her suitors, but this was the first and only time that she had been happy to do it. Fortunately, Dawn kept a perfectly clean house up there, where the sun didn't shine. As the newly subservient vixen finished milking the remaining sperm from his dick, Reuben trembled in chills and goose bumps, as his penis had never felt so tender or sensitive. His sperm tasted salty, while yet somehow sweet, at the same time. The submissive Dawn suckled at her new Master's penis, as if it were a pacifier that she had grown emotionally attached to.

Once they had both caught their second wind, they realized that they were pressing their luck by staying naked from the waist down. They quickly hurried to put their pants back on, before giving their sexual serendipity a chance to run out. Before Dawn could chase after her pants, Reuben retrieved them for her, showing his gentleman side.

Dawn was physically alluring, as if her body had been created for sin. It was a toss-up, which was more gorgeous, her face or her figure. She was picture perfect, but only on the exterior. Men who would have been good for her, were either too intimidated to talk to her or were uninterested because of her reputation, and men who were damaging to her…only used her for her magnificent and sensual body. She found herself wondering where Reuben would fall on that scale, or if he would prove to be somewhere on the borderline. Her face was that of an angel, though she behaved like a horny little devil. Her curves were all in the right place, combined with her seductive, slender physique.

Reuben now sat beside her, on her bed. They both hung their head, not in shame, but in mutual fear that the other would now lose interest in them. The silence was so loud, that you could hear a single pin drop on a shag carpet.

"I'm sorry," Reuben said, being the first to break the ice, but still avoiding making awkward eye contact.

"For what?" Dawn asked, still embarrassed that he saw her overly hairy lower half.

"I forced myself on you," Reuben said.

"No," she denied any protest, now looking at him, and putting her reassuring hand on his quivering leg, "You didn't, not at all. I wanted it. I wanted you. Besides," she added, "I'm the one who should be sorry."

"Why?" he asked, confused.

"You saw me. You saw my ugliness," she answered, referring to her excessive hair growth on her body.

"Dawn," he said back, in an adoring and amorous voice, "That's crazy, girl. Don't talk like that, baby. You're shick. You're the most blazin' thing I've ever seen."

Dawn moved her warm hand from his less heated inner thigh, and took his clammy hand into hers. She put his refrigerated hand under her button-snapped shirt, and moved it up to her perfectly smooth, succulent breasts, and then to her armpits, which were anything but. Reuben felt unusually long and abnormally coarse hair coming from her forest-like armpits. Reuben understood why Dawn felt so self-conscious, but still strongly argued her belief that it made her unattractive or even undesirable.

"See," she said, as her lower jaw began to quiver and her eyes started to water. "I'm a dog."

"No," Reuben immediately rebutted, shaking his head in disagreement, "You're not. So what if you have excessive body hair? I don't care about that. It doesn't make you any less dreamy to me. It doesn't make you any less you."

"You haven't been skinny dipping with me," she noted, as if deliberately trying to scare him off or push him away, feeling a bit repulsive, insignificant, and unworthy of his compulsive obsession and devoted affections.

"I don't dig what you're saying, baby?" Reuben admitted, not understanding why, or comprehending how, skinny-dipping with her would or could ever be a bad thing.

"It gets much worse" she claimed. "There's more to see. Besides, I smell like a wet dog, when my hair gets wet."

"If you feel that strongly about it, why don't you shave it off?" Reuben asked, still trying earnestly to console her, but also diligently attempting to now solve her problem, which he felt was purely cosmetic and still didn't bother him in the least, or change the way he felt about her. "If you like" he added, "I could trim your hairs and shave your body for you. I'd be happy to help you with that, if it would make things easier on you."

"You're very sweet, but I've tried," she said, "It doesn't work. As soon as I cut it off, it grows back, before the night falls and the day is over." Reuben saw that tears of sorrow were rushing down her angelic face, as she was talking to him, now with her head hung in shame, "When it grows back…which is almost instantly, it grows back longer and thicker, so I eventually had to just stop trying to get rid of it, and just learn to tolerate it."

"Dawn," Reuben began, now laying his chilled hand on her toasty inner thigh, "It doesn't bother me, and it shouldn't bother you. It's just hair; it doesn't change who you are, and certainly doesn't change my covetous hankering for you." Reuben brought his other hand up to her soft face, and began gently rubbing her moist chin and cheeks. "I don't see any hair growth up here," he said, trying to comfort her and get her to finally see herself as he saw her. "You're absolutely stunning, Dawn, body hair or no body hair. You don't have any on your face, baby…not even a faint mustache, so be thankful for that."

"You're not stuttering anymore," Dawn said grinning, pointing out that Reuben had clearly become relaxed and comfortable with his dream lover.

Reuben blushed, and looked again at the hard ground, embarrassed that he had stammered so badly before, in front of his muse. Dawn placed her silky hand on the back of his redhead, and gently guided him down to her lap, so that his ginger-head was resting on her, and his body was laying on its side, beside her, on the bed.

"I've never been in the lap of luxury before," he told her, as she lovingly stroked his crimson hair, as if to nurture him into her heart. "I don't dig why you feel so hideous," Reuben told her, "If you could see what I see, you would never say such a slander about yourself."

"I'm glad that you see that in me," she replied. "For what it's worth, I think you're beautiful too, Reuben. You're a good man, and have a great heart."

"You don't have to say that," Reuben said, knowing all-too-well that he was the antithesis of beauty.

"I know I don't have to," she responded. "I love your spirit."

"I'm ghastly odious," Reuben said, having accepted the cursed hand that God had so cruelly dealt him, from birth. "I'm repugnant. I'm a monster."

"No," Dawn disagreed, "I don't think so," she said in a soft and tender voice, as she moved her caring hand down to stroke his rough face. Dawn then touched between his partially chapped lips, with her index finger...then gently rubbing and massaging his upper hair lip.

Reuben quickly grabbed her hand, not to hurt her, but to kiss the tip of her finger.

"You're very kind, Dawn," Reuben said, "but I know otherwise. I'm a beast."

"They say that you're only as old as you feel" Dawn told him. "Well, I also believe that you're only a monster if your heart is black, and I see a heart of gold in you...not a heart of stone. I see such groovy love in your charming but depressed eyes."

"If there is anything redeemable about me, or any love in my broken heart, it's only because of you," Reuben replied back, swallowing his own acidic saliva, as he fought not to break down and cry in front of the love of his otherwise miserable life.

"I don't really even know you, but yet I..." Dawn began to confide, but couldn't muster up the courage it took to finish.

"I know," he graciously interrupted, with the intent of sparing her, "I feel the same about you."

Dawn noticed that something was bothering him. Something was troubling his mind, and she could see it as clear as if it had been written all over his face. "What, baby?" she asked. "What's wrong?"

"I don't want to lose you" Reuben answered. "I just found you. I don't want to lose you."

"Baby" she said in a reaffirming voice, "I'm not going anywhere." Dawn misinterpreted his fear, assuming he was suddenly doubting her commitment to him. "I'm not leaving you, Reuben. I'm here for as long as you want me, baby."

"It's not you" he said back, "It's God."

"I don't understand," she admitted.

"The Lord giveth and the Lord taketh away" Reuben quoted. "That's the Bible. What the Scriptures don't say, however, is that the Lord really enjoys the latter part. Taking away is the Lord's favorite thing."

"The Bible also tells us that God blesses the pure of heart," she added. "I know the Bible too, baby. Sadly, I know it well enough to know that many parts of it aren't as true as I'd like them to be. Many of the promises made in the Bible only seem to cater to the worst people."

"God doesn't bless the pure of heart" Reuben corroborated. "He blesses the heartless."

"I know, baby" she vouched. "I know. But...the Lord won't put anything or anyone between us. I won't let him. I promise. You're stuck with me, baby" she vowed. "Forever, baby. I'm yours...forever."

The two romantic lovers looked down, and saw that they were unknowingly holding hands. Just then, one of the male nurses barged in and interrupted their time of bonding.

"What the fuck are you doing in here?" Nurse Carl asked, having his own perverse suspicions. "You both know the fucking rules. There is no mixing of genders in these sleeping quarters!"

"We were just talking," Dawn said quickly, to protect her newfound soulmate from any punishment or consequence.

"Yeah," Reuben chivalrously backed her up, as he promptly sat up and adjusted himself so that he was sitting on the side of the bed next to Dawn, instead of still resting on her lap. "Just getting to know each other."

"We were just mellowing" Dawn added, "You know, just taking it easy."

"Well, you two can do that in the communal areas of the ward, not in each other's rooms. These rooms are for reflecting and resting, not socializing and fraternizing."

Reuben, not wanting to get Dawn in any more trouble than he already had, politely got up and left, without so much as a verbal *goodbye* to her, and obediently returned to his assigned cell. Reuben was pleased to find that Joshua wasn't around, when he stepped through their door. Frustrated, he laid on his stomach, using his folded arm as a hard pillow under his head. Just as he began to relax and calm down, he heard an unexpected knock at the door. Getting up, he went to investigate whom it was, presuming that it was one of the staff members coming to harass him about something petty. Opening the door, he saw that it was William, who had come to pay him an unannounced visit.

"What it is, brother," William said, "You have a minute?"

"Um, sure, I guess," Reuben answered in curiosity, not sure what this was all about.

"Can I come in?" William asked permission. "I just think we should talk."

"Right on," Reuben agreed. "Enlighten me. What's on your mind?" he asked William, getting the vibe from him that whatever he had to get off his chest was of importance.

William walked in with equal amounts of hesitation and obligation, and sat on the edge of the lower bunk bed, while Reuben cautiously shut the door behind him.

"What's on your mind, William?" Reuben asked again.

"Look, Reuben. I'm not here to psyche you, burn you, or mess with your head. I know you and Dawn have gotten very close," William bluntly began, seeing the distressed look on Reuben's face and noticing that he started to defensively make fists with his hands. "It's not like that," William added, "I'm not here to judge either of you, or try to scare you away from her. In fact, I think it's far out that you two have found each other," he said, while Reuben relaxed, exhaled, and unclenched his hands.

"I appreciate that," Reuben said. "I'd also be grateful if you could kindly keep this between us. They've kind of been giving us a hard time, and I don't want to cause Dawn any more trouble than I already have."

"I'm down with that. I'm not going to tell anyone," William replied. "I haven't told anyone. You two have a good vibe going, and I have no desire to come between that or fuck that up. Look, man, I'm here only because I feel that I need to clue you in a bit more about what you've gotten yourself into."

"I'm not sure I get your meaning?" Reuben asked inquisitively, not quite certain how to take that.

"Dawn's a groovy chick. She is. She's something special. I've heard a lot of people call her an airhead, but she's not. Did she tell you about her past? Has she shared that with you at all? By that, I mean, has she opened up to you more than she has with the rest of us?"

"If you mean sexually…if that's what you're referring to…she's not like that anymore," Reuben said in her defense. "She's committed herself to me, and I trust her…I trust her" he repeated aloud, trying to not only convince William, but himself as well.

"No, it's not that," William replied. "I'm here to tell you about what her Uncle did."

"Her Uncle?"

"Yeah, on her mother's side. Her father isn't the only one who has issues. Dawn's Uncle went total bananas on these older kids, when Dawn was just a child. Dawn was visiting her cousins in the Sterling suburbs. This family lived in a cul de sac, within view of the Elementary school. Her two cousins, who were 8 and 3 at the time, were out riding their *Big Wheels*. Their neighbors, who lived directly across from their house, had three sons who were either close to finishing High School, or had already graduated. These nasty neighbors weren't the best people, and had been harassing Dawn's relatives for quite some time, about…and over…trivial matters. These sadistic people had even maliciously trapped their cat at one point, and tried to have it put down. Anyway, these teenagers saw through their windows, that Dawn's two cousins were out playing in the center of the cul de sac. Within minutes, these guys had phoned their buddies, and next thing you knew, they were all out riding their 10 speed *Schwinn* and *Huffy* bikes."

"What happened?" Reuben asked, anxious to hear the end of the story.

"Dawn's Aunt saw what was happening through their windows, and saw these teenagers come within mere inches of crushing their two young boys. The younger of the two boys, literally almost got run over, as he tended to stop his *Big Wheel*, and reach down to pick up bottle caps he'd find in the street. Just as the little boy did this very thing, one of the teenagers popped a wheelie, and when his bike landed, it came dangerously close to flattening the little boy's head. As she screamed for her sons, their father...Dawn's Uncle...had run downstairs to go out the door, and charged after them. Dawn watched nervously through their picture window, as her Uncle knocked every one of those teenagers off their bikes, and brutally beat them to a bloody pulp, introducing their prideful faces to the rock-hard asphalt."

"Wow," Reuben said, "That's heavy. Did Dawn's Uncle get pinched?"

"Oh yeah," William said. "He spent some time in prison for first degree murder and aggravated assault, which included killing one and putting three others in intensive care. Look, Reuben...the point is, Dawn saw this happen...and at a very impressionable age. It was just one more afflicted notch on the laundry list of adversity moments that have inevitably and tragically traumatized her. She's suffered a very hard...very painful...life. Knowing her as long as I have, I'd say she's one tick away from exploding, much like how her Uncle did, in front of her."

"Well," Reuben said, "It sounds to me like her Uncle was justified in what he did, even if he did end up snuffing one of those teenagers."

"I don't agree. I don't think violence can ever be solved with more violence," William argued, "and though he certainly had valid reason for viciously attacking those kids, it doesn't change the fact that he had it inside of him to do more. Her Uncle is just one of the many people in Dawn's life, who have influenced her in a destructive way."

Reuben just slowly shook his head, and though he understood that William meant well, it still angered him that he was bad mouthing Dawn, even if it was subliminal or unintentional.

"I know a lot of guys look at me like I'm a square," William continued, "but I could really use a toke off a fucking doobie right about now...or even a taste of one of those special brownies."

"Really? I thought you were a Jesus freak," Reuben said, surprised at his peer's bold statement.

"Oh, I am," William immediately confirmed.

"But you swear, and smoke reefer?" Reuben asked, just to make sure that he wasn't delusional or somehow hallucinating this part of their conversation.

"Don't kid yourself," William said in response. "Jesus was the hippest hippy in the bunch, man. Think about it. Every painting you see of Christ, he has long hair. He wore cheap rags for clothes, so he clearly didn't care about fashion or materialism. The Bible makes it clear that he was hated and hunted by the government, because they felt threatened by him. Jesus came to bring peace, love, and mercy to all he came across. He cared for others more than he valued himself, even though he was the Son of God. He accepted and befriended those who were different or lost. He walked around barefoot, half the time, protesting injustice and preaching love. Wouldn't you call that a hippy?"

"Wow, yeah" Reuben answered, "that actually makes a lot of sense. I never looked at Jesus that way, William. That's a very intriguing analysis of the Messiah."

"John Lennon is the Walrus, who believes that people are naturally good, if they just believe in love. Jesus Christ was the Lamb, who believed that people are inherently wicked, but are worth saving. They both love mankind, and want only peace and love for the world, man. Can you dig it?" William asked, grinning like the basket case he was.

Meanwhile, Dawn had begun to feel claustrophobic alone in her room, from the separation anxiety she instantaneously felt from the evolving doubt on whether or not they were going to make their relationship work, despite all the obstacles that were blocking their progress. Though it would have been easy to crash on her bed and curl up into a ball, she decided to go for a stroll and sulk while being mobile. As she wandered without direction, through the mental health facility, with her chin hanging low and her eyes focused on the floor, she literally and inadvertently bumped into Nurse Monica.

"Oh, shit!" Nurse Monica said, as she nearly fell over backwards, and tripping over her own feet.

"Fuck," Dawn said, realizing what she had done. "I'm so sorry, Nurse Monica."

"Its fine, sweetie. It's okay. It was an accident," Nurse Monica relieved her, as she regained her balance and collected herself.

Out of the blue, Dawn began to completely break down emotionally, sobbing and weeping in front of the friendly nurse.

"Oh my God...Dawn...what's wrong?" Nurse Monica asked, genuinely concerned. "Are you okay?

Sweetie? What's the matter, hun? Did something happen?"

Nurse Monica outstretched her arms and stepped up to Dawn, wrapping her arms around her back, pulling her towards her. Dawn cried in her chest, as Nurse Monica hugged her tight and gently stroked the back of her head, doing what she could to console her. Though Dawn wasn't talking or confiding in her, Nurse Monica was attentive enough to sense that something was causing her pain…something that she didn't feel safe to unveil. She could feel Dawn's heart race and her body tremor.

"Dawn," she said softly, so that only Dawn could hear, "I'm here for you, sweetheart. Whatever it is, I'm here for you. It's okay to talk to me, if you decide you want to. It's safe to talk to me."

"I love him," Dawn told her in a whimpering whisper. "I love him."

"Oh, honey…sweetie," Nurse Monica said in response. "It's okay. It will be okay," she added, not sure who Dawn was talking about, but felt for her all the same, seeing how torn up she was about him. As both staff and patient passed by them, they continued to stand in place together, holding each other, for several more minutes, as if for that brief period of time…they were the only two people left that existed.

Hours later, Reuben and Dawn were deliberately making a conscious effort to stay clear from one another, for appearances sake, hoping that it might dispel any further potential interference or interdiction. It was unbearably painful being apart, but they agreed telepathically, to wait until they could get out of there, before resuming their hot n' heavy, committed courtship. Dawn had awoken something in him, something that could never be extinguished or replaced. Reuben, for the first time in his life, felt alive. He thought back on what it felt like to be inside her, remembering how he would pump her hard and fast, and then return to going slow and taking his time. Reuben watched from a safe distance, staring unobtrusively at her delectably luscious ass, when a hand that wasn't hers touched his aching shoulder.

"You know she's just above the age of consent, right?" Nurse Carl said, at a volume exclusive for Reuben's ears alone, "You're chasing what was not long ago, jailbait, Charlie. This isn't going to end well, for either one of you."

"Not that I'm guilty of your allegation," Reuben said, "But you people are the last ones who should be preaching against cradle robbing or abusing authority." Reuben turned, and looked his accuser in the eyes, "I suggest, Nurse Carl, that if you wish to keep your job and your health, that you leave her alone. My name is Reuben, by the way, not Charlie."

"I'm sure I don't know what you're talking about," Nurse Carl equivocated, with the denotation of charlatan scribbled all over his pudgy face, "I'm happily married and a doting father of three children. I have no interest in throwing all that away for a whore like your little bitch."

"Okay," Reuben said, "Let's do without the pleasantries, shall we. I realize you see yourself as this smooth operator, who can't be touched, but...you're only fooling yourself if you think I fall for your sanctimonious manipulation. With that in mind, say whatever helps you sleep at night, just keep your filthy hands off of her."

"Or what?" Nurse Carl asked, getting right in Reuben's pale face, as if to try and either intimidate him or kiss him. "Boy, you best keep stepping. I'm a US Marine. I can tear you up, like you were a sheet of tissue paper."

"What's going on here?" Nurse Monica stepped in, discerning that something was terribly amiss.

"Nothing," Nurse Carl deceptively asserted. "Just friendly banter between staff and patient."

"Yeah," Reuben regretfully conceded, just to avoid continued complication and interrogation, "No major indiscretion or altercation to speak of," he knowingly lied, not foreseeing that it was much bigger than he had originally interpreted it to be, and that this would ultimately and inevitably lead to an unfavorable outcome for both himself and his first love.

Reuben shamelessly walked away, not wanting to rock the boat further, by ripping out Nurse Carl's putrid slime orb that he magically masqueraded as something resembling a heart. Reuben had no doubt that he would commit bloody murder, in order to protect his newfound love, but it just wasn't worth it, if it wasn't necessary. He had an endgame in mind, and that was to build a new life with Dawn, which would become even more impractical, if he were forever condemned behind bars. He wouldn't be much good for her, if he could never lay with her under the comforting blanket of the night sky.

OCTOBER 31, 1977

It was 3AM, and all of the convalescents were fast asleep, except for Reuben, or so he thought. He had only been there for a workweek, but it had begun to feel like longer than a millennium. Dawn had certainly made his stay more bearable, but on the other hand, this ever-growing newfound love that he attained in her, was now taking its toll on him. He wanted to break free from the confines of their psychiatric penitentiary, and he needed to take Dawn with him. He had no viable plan on where they would go, or how they would survive, and his parlous susceptibility to the sun's poisonous radiation wasn't going to make their quest of passion any easier. He obviously wouldn't be able to move in with her, and he couldn't invite her to live with him at his pad, as his parents would never let him have anything in the cellar that brought him so much happiness. He didn't know what they would do, or how they would do it, but he knew that she was the one, and he had no intention of ever giving up on her or letting her go, knowing that if he did, he would spend the rest of his miserable eternity regretting it and agonizing over his loss.

Dawn, incapable of forgetting about Reuben and dying to be held by him again, couldn't manage to fall asleep either. Deciding to tolerate a cold shower, foolishly tricking herself into believing it would alleviate her relentless yearning; she put on her fluffy blue slippers, and left her room, heading toward the communal lavatory. Walking passed the nurses' desk; she wasn't marginally surprised, but refreshingly relieved to see that nobody was at their station. She figured that whichever staff member was on shift was either making their rounds or curled up asleep somewhere in the facility. She was just thrilled that they weren't coming to her door, for once. When Dawn finally made it to the shared shower stall, she heard the water running. She quietly stepped into the bath area, which was sadly much larger than their sleeping quarters, and saw through the steam, that someone was in there. Reuben preferred taking hot showers, as the thick steam always provided a smokescreen of sorts, so he wouldn't have to look at himself as closely. He was pleased to find that there were no mirrors in the communal bath area either, since the hospital was too concerned about losing a patient to broken glass, and thereby suffering the legal hell afterwards. Reuben just finished rinsing the soap out of his eyes, and happened to notice and recognize her familiar shadow through the cut-rate, white curtain.

"Dawn?" he called out with hope, in just above an audible whisper. "Is that you?"

Dawn slowly pulled open the cheap shower curtain, and once again faced the enchanted, yet complicated, love of her life. She had already disrobed, and was more than ready to join him.

"You shouldn't be here," Reuben said, worried that they would get caught, and would in turn, directly endanger her.

"Do you really want me to go?" she asked him...already knowing his answer...giving him a pouty, puppy-dog mien while deliberately speaking in a baby-type voice, while she tilted her head down and manipulatively batted her big, beautiful blue eyes.

Reuben, against his better judgment, opened wide his unconditional arms to her, and the illuminatingly radiant Dawn joyously stepped in to join him, carefully closing the discounted curtain behind her. Locked in a tender embrace, they held each other for several minutes without saying a word, caressing and exploring one another. Dawn felt both fresh cuts and old scars all over his aching back. Tears rolled and streamed down her empathetic face, mixing with the hot water from the showerhead, as she genuinely hurt for her cherished companion. She could relate to his haunting pain, enough to keep her from asking him to reveal any more details about the nature or origin of his wounds. She figured he would share more with her in time, if and when he was ready. As Reuben reached around and affectionately kneaded her back, while he was holding her close, he felt a mane of coarse hair (about three inches long) that seemed to begin at the crest of the spine of her neck, and ended just above the gothic tramp stamp which permanently hovered over the crack of her ass. Reuben understood why she kept the hair on her head at the length she did, as it concealed the brisk hair on her neck and back rather effectively. Other than this mane aligning the center of her spine, the rest of her back felt as smooth as a baby's tush, and he still continued to see her as the embodiment of his prayers. Reuben loved her with everything inside of him, and nothing was ever going to change that. His prayers were always brutally and blatantly ignored, that was until God graced him with Dawn. He was so afraid of God being an Indian giver that he was fully prepared to sacrifice the fate of his own soul to keep her in his arms.

"You never answered my question," Dawn said in a muffled voice, with her hot mouth pressed against his albino chest.

"What was that, baby?" Reuben asked, not recalling at the moment, which question she was currently referring to.

The slender yet voluptuous Dawn delicately pushed herself from his chest, using her flat palms on his middle-aged gut, so she could look her best friend in the eye.

"Would you like to kiss me?" she asked him again.

With that, Reuben slowly leaned inward, and met her waiting lips halfway, soon sharing a kiss of intimacy that would redefine the meaning of passion. Their thirsty tongues explored one another, as if touring each other's tonsils, there in the communal shower stall. The steamy shower was refreshing, but not because they hadn't run out of warm water.

"I'm utterly mesmerized by you," he said. "You are what I have waited for...for so long...even before I knew I had been waiting for you."

"I can't be without you," Dawn said back. "You are my every breath. You make me feel safe, Reuben. I don't know why or how exactly, but you do."

"You do realize that I'm old enough to be your father, right?" Reuben asked, not wanting her to abandon him, but at the same time trying desperately to ground himself in some level of reality again, for both of their sakes. "I mean, I'm no young blood. Are you sure you want to be with me?" he asked, worried about little things like the possibility of erectile dysfunction and heart failure, because of his seasoned age and because he had already lived much longer than he was medically expected to.

"I believe kismet brought us together," Dawn answered him. "You are my kindred spirit. My soulmate. I'm never going to let you go or throw you away...unless you tell me to. Please don't tell me to. I need you, Daddy...Daddy-O."

Reuben, because of his incurable disease, had repellant armpit odor that he couldn't manage or maintenance. His bleached skin had an aversion to any and all forms of deodorant. In fact, the only laundry detergent he could handle without issues was *Ivory Snow*. When the desirable Dawn took the bar of *Coast* soap off the small shelf (which was gripped onto the shower liner), she dropped it, as it had managed to slip right out of her silky hand.

"I'll get it," she said, as she bent down in front of him, brushing the top of her head against his penis, on the way down.

Dawn saw, for the first time, that he had no toenails. As Dawn straightened her back, she sniffed and French-kissed his semi-erect penis, on her way back up. Now standing before him again, she handed the bar soap to Reuben. When she did so, he briefly feared that she was trying to subtly hint at something.

"Would you do the honors, Daddy?" she asked, in her irresistible, adolescent voice.

As Reuben took his time thoroughly washing and scrubbing her envied body of lust, Dawn gently closed her ocean-blue eyes, and thought to herself how far she had come, since first meeting him. Though she had behaved like a promiscuous harlot, she had never removed any article of clothing that wasn't absolutely necessary to accomplish the dirty deed. So, though there were many horny men who came to know her in the biblical sense, none had ever seen her in her full birthday suit, other than him and her degenerate father. Though she had lived like a slut for so long, she had remained inhibited in certain ways…that was until now. Whether anyone knew it or not, Dawn was repulsed by being a whore, but she was used to it and had accepted that it was expected of her. Even though she had been around the block more than her share, she wasn't proud of it and never had any feelings behind it that weren't nauseating. Reuben had been the first and only one, besides her biological Daddy, to completely see her in the full flesh…and the only one to be up her ass. Reuben knelt down behind her, and washed her delicious ass, with his sudsy hands. He had brought a washcloth to the shower with him, but hadn't used it on her, as it would take away from the fun of showering with his one true love.

"Slap me some skin, Daddy?" she asked him.

"What?" Reuben questioned her, not sure what she meant by her request, and not wanting to assume anything when he may be wrong.

"Spank me," she promptly cleared up any misconception or misunderstanding. "Since you're down there, give me a good slap on the ass. You know you want to," she added seductively.

Though this tempted Reuben to an extent, he didn't wish to do anything that had the potential of hurting her, and couldn't live with accidentally messing it up or hitting her too hard, and therefore scaring her away and losing his one and only chance at love.

"Spank me, Daddy," she insisted. "It's alright. You won't break me."

Though she had gone beyond the call of duty to prove her irrefutable love for him, Reuben still couldn't get past how easy she was on the eyes, and how bewildered he was to be the lucky recipient of such undying, unconditional love. He wasn't complaining, by any means, but just couldn't understand how she could choose to give her priceless love to a beast like him.

Once Reuben had cleaned Dawn, so meticulously that one could eat off of her, she graciously returned the favor, pleasing him by devoting particular and scrupulous attention to his penile section. Before long, the two lovers were embracing again, holding each other as tight and as close as humanly possible, as if it were quite literally their last chance to do so. Dawn was only 5'7," to Reuben's six-foot-three stature, so her head rested on his chest, which he didn't exactly mind. He continued holding her for as long as he could, while the showerhead kept spraying warm water on their naturally heated bodies. Eventually, the water temperature began to go frigid, which was their cue to go back to bed and warm each other up by other means.

"I'll go first," Dawn said. "Listen for me."

"My hearing isn't that good, baby," Reuben responded. "My vision, unfortunately, isn't so reliable these days either."

Reuben could see her well enough, but he kept the fact that he was legally blind, to himself. His eyes worked, but not nearly as well as he would have liked. He often had to squint to see, especially when trying to read. His vision was blurred, and was much worse on certain days, or first thing in the morning. The only time he could see fairly well was in the dark, which somehow worked better for him.

"No, sweetheart," she said, "I meant listen for me here," she repeated, as she reached up and gently tapped the middle of his forehead. "We've spoken telepathically before, Daddy. Our special connection is obviously much stronger and deeper than we think."

"Okay," Reuben nodded in compliance, "but I think we've connected more here," he said as he gently touched her in the center of her chest, right between her youthful and ample bosom.

Dawn smiled fondly at her *magic man*, before making her way back to her room. She could see that the staff nurse, stuck with the graveyard duty, had returned to her desk, but that she had once again chosen to join her shift mates on catching up on some indubitably deprived sleep. Once Dawn was theoretically safe in her room, she psychically summoned her beloved Reuben. He was once again keeping and enjoying her company, mere minutes later. Without even having to ask, the two intimate strangers began slow dancing, to music that wasn't actually playing and that only they could hear.

"Are you going to take me to a night club, when we get out?" she asked him.

"I suppose that's a possible option," he answered. "Just as long as we don't stay out too close to sunrise. My skin can't handle prolonged exposure to the solar radiation."

"I'd like to boogie with you sometime, at a roller disco or something," she said, "I think that would be pretty groovy. Or, not…honestly, it wouldn't matter what we'd do or where we'd go…just as long as we are together."

"Dawn," he said, "I should really get back to my own room now. We don't want to risk being seen mauling each other like this. I don't know how many strikes we're going to get before Nurse Carl manifests his wrath in ways we'd rather not be around to see…or worse, not be able to recover from. If anything bad ever happened to you, and I wasn't there to…I…I don't know what I…"

"I know," she agreed, touched that he loved her that much. "I know, Daddy. I can dig what you're saying.

Just hold me for a few minutes, while I fall asleep. Please, Daddy," she begged, showing her sweet but addictive co-dependency even further.

"I'm pretty tired too," he admitted. He remembered how he would sleep through the day, and how it was the only time that he could dream of a different and better life...one where he wasn't abundantly cursed and forsaken by God, and not afflicted with permanent sickness, ugliness, inadequacy, isolation and rejection. Those days were over now, and he only had her to thank. He was undeniably dependent on her love, for his very survival.

Reuben accommodated her wishes and laid with her in the hospital bed, which was strangely significantly more comfortable than the one he had been given to sleep on. He had every intention of retiring to his own room, the second he felt Dawn begin to dose off. However, much like how truck drivers convince themselves that they can stay alert through fatigue, Reuben was only setting himself up for a rude awakening.

"You're not inadequate," she said, successfully reading his mind. "You're not ugly. You're not alone anymore, and for what it's worth, I need you, Daddy. I'm very dependent on you...and I certainly will never reject or replace you."

Little did Reuben realize that he had good reason to worry about losing her, as lightning never struck twice.

Dawn, unlike most young women, actually meant her vows and had no selfish or deceptive agenda behind them. Being so close to her like this, they couldn't abstain from making out again, as if it were second nature at this point to submit to the irresistible temptation. Going at it like a pair of sex junkies, they impatiently removed each other's clothes, like rabid dogs in heat, and Reuben slipped inside of her...this time entering her bloody vagina. Dawn remained on her back this time, while Reuben experimented with the classic missionary position, which was highly appropriate, considering the words to come out of his mouth shortly thereafter.

"Oh god...oh god...I'm sorry, baby" Reuben told her, as his breath grew faster and heavier. "But since our first time together, all I can ever think about is scoring with you."

"It's okay, Daddy," she said, "I want to be your end zone. Jump my bones, Daddy," she begged. "Let me get on top though," she asked; now breathing as heavily as her male suitor. "I want to ride you. I want to sit on it," she pleaded, like a stoner who desperately needed a fix.

"No," Reuben immediately denied her, "The only thing you're allowed to ride is my face. You'll get it from behind, or this way, but I'll be the one taking control," Reuben said, while he playfully reached up and squeezed her mouth, pushing her pouty lips together in a vertical way.

Starting off slow and gentle, he progressively got faster and harder. He wanted so badly to savor the feeling and hold in his cum, to prolong the duration of the intercourse, but she didn't make it very easy. As he pounded away at her wet pussy, like there was no tomorrow, the shaking of the mattress pushed out her silver flask, which she had been keeping underneath. Reuben heard it hit the stone floor, but continued making love to her, until they inevitably came together this time. As the sweaty Dawn continued moaning and panting from their mutual climax, Reuben, who was also perspired, rolled over to the edge of her bed, and reached down to the floor with his arm.

"What's this?" he asked her, showing her the flask he now held in his hand.

"I haven't taken a swig since we...Well, since you sodomized me," she lied, embarrassed to have her self-destructive vice discovered, by the last person she wanted to find out.

"Look, Dawn," Reuben started, in a soothing voice, "I'm not judging you, hun. I'd be a hypocrite if I did. I mean, the way I crave you, could very easily and fairly be called an addiction. We all have them. Just, please, don't let it drown you. You're so young yet...and you shouldn't be touching this stuff. I'm not judging you, I'm just worried about you."

"I know, Daddy," she said. "I know you're worried about me, but I'm okay. I appreciate your concern though. It makes me feel warm inside to know that you care so much about me."

"I just don't want to lose you," he said, "especially to something like terminal liver damage."

"You won't, I promise," she pledged, unsure herself if she could really keep that oath, "I just used the liquor to numb the pain." Hearing herself say this, she realized that her reason...though honest and justified...wasn't painting her in such a good light.

"You don't have to feel pain anymore," he told her, "You have me now. I'm here for you baby, if you'll just let me in."

"I know," she said, "and you are in."

Dawn took the silver flask from his hand, and rolled him back on his back. She put the flask under her pillow, in hopes that he would somehow magically forget that he even saw it. She positioned herself next to Reuben, so that she was lying on her stomach, and her face was over his shoulder. Using her hand to take his arm and lift it over his head, she began licking his armpit, lapping it like a dog. Reuben was staggered by this, but didn't do anything to stop her. As obscurely taboo as this was, it was actually pretty kinky, and felt oddly pleasurable.

"I should have done this before the shower," she said, astounding him even more. "You would have tasted better."

"I wish I had a dozen red roses," Reuben told her, "If I did, I would pick off all the pedals and spread them all over your bed, before lying you down on it."

"Wow," she said, overcome with his thoughtful romantic gesture, "Though I appreciate the sweet sentiment, Daddy, I'm kind of glad you don't have those red roses."

"Why?" he asked. "Too much?" he inquired; worried that maybe he had tried too hard or taken things too far somehow.

"No. It's not that. It's really very sweet that you even want to do that for me, but...I'm highly allergic to roses. I'm deathly allergic to them. It's actually quite a nightmare. I break out in hives, and swell up, and if it's untreated for too long, I eventually can't breathe. Last time I came into direct contact with red roses, my parents had to rush me to the local Emergency Room."

Reuben got very comfortable with her on the bed, and let Dawn rest her head on his bare chest, as she looked down at his blood soaked penis. Reuben stroked her hair this time, while she twirled and played with the scraggly hairs that were sprawled out on his white chest.

"Tell me something about you that I don't know," she asked, eager to know all she could about him, and as soon as possible, as if their days together were numbered.

"When I was young, I never left the house," he told her. "I couldn't. It was more dangerous for me out there than it was living under my parents roof."

"Were you home schooled?" she asked, not sure she understood what he meant.

"Not quite in the way you'd expect. I got an education, but it wasn't an academic one. My parents were ashamed of me. My mother often told me that she wished she had lost me in a miscarriage. She'd stand by, and look the other way, while my father beat me mercilessly with his leather belt. He'd put these black leather gloves on, tie my wrists with barbwire, and then wallop on my body, taking out the anger on me that he felt for himself, for having such a hideous son. My mother used to watch him pulverize me, and then while I laid there bleeding, she'd lay a wooden crucifix on my chest or sprinkle my body with 'blessed water' that she would steal from our church, and tell me she'd *pray for me*. They were committed Catholics, and believed me to be some sort of curse from God, as punishment for their past unforgiven transgressions. They didn't even have to pawn me off as being a scooby, since they knew I'd never leave the cellar. There were crucifixes hanging on the walls, throughout the house, even down in the basement, where I spent most of my life. My parents also verbally crucified me for wearing black all the time. Yet, they were the ones to buy my threads, since I couldn't venture outside and take care of myself. I was a burden, because I was too dependent on them, for my needs. The most color I've ever worn was the faded blue on my hand-me-down denim. They made me feel like there was something wrong with me, because I was drawn to darkness, when it was God who made me this way. They were also the ones who put black light bulbs in the cellar."

"Why didn't you runaway?" she asked him.

"I thought about it, even fantasized about it, but it just wasn't in the cards. My blood disorder made life significantly difficult. It's what makes me look like this. It also makes me dangerously sensitive to ultraviolet rays. My father was prone to skin cancer, and was always back and forth to the doctor to have it removed. My mother was anemic. It didn't take much effort for her to hurt herself, and when she bled, she bled quickly and profusely. Because of this, she was very dependent on my father for nearly everything. My mother was never faithful to my father, but he didn't really care as long as she continued to come home to him. She was physically lush, but cold around the heart. He was financially wealthy, as a successful criminal attorney."

"Is your condition fatal?" Dawn asked him, worried that his illness may take him from her. "I mean...is this...will this condition of yours get worse?"

"From what I've read about porphyria, there's a good chance that, the longer I live with this, the higher the odds that I will eventually have to resort to drinking blood, just to keep me sane, and breathing," Reuben answered.

"You would never hurt me," Dawn said, trying to convince them both of her wishful thinking.

"Of course not," he reassured her. "If it ever gets to the point of no return, we'll find a way to live with it. I just might need you to trap small animals for me," Reuben said with a smirk, trying to make light of the subject, and ease her concern. "If you don't mind me asking," he said, trying to veer the emphasis back on her, "what makes your body hair the way it is?"

"I have what's called Hypertrichosis, also known as the Ambras Syndrome. Some cases happen to the person later in life. Mine was congenital. This disorder is more often found in males, and only in rare cases found in females. Mine is also highly unusual, because in most cases, the person isn't affected in the pubic region, but is affected in the face. It's the exact opposite in my situation. Thank God for small favors, huh?"

"God hasn't done either one of us any favors. You said, in group, that you believe you're here because you assaulted someone?" he began. "Why here, instead of jail? I mean no offense. I'm just curious. You don't have to answer, if..."

"No, it's okay," she said, "They say it was the way I went about it. I chased the guy, and pounced on him. They found severe scratches and deep cuts on his body. I also bit him in the neck, which was what landed him in the ER. The doctor who gave me the psychiatric evaluation diagnosed me as suffering from lycanthropy?"

"Lycanthropy? The fictional disease that causes one to become a werewolf?"

"Actually," Dawn said smiling, "Lycanthropy is originally an ancient medical term, used to describe a mentally ill person who believes, in their delusional state, that they can transform into an animal."

"Do you believe that you can change shape, and become an animal?" Reuben asked.

"I don't think I can change shape, but I think I've proven to you that I can be an animal...at least in bed, right?"

Reuben smiles, and nods his head, as if to blush.

"It's just a label, sweetie," she added. "Let them think what they want. People will believe what they want. It doesn't mean that it has to affect us or our life."

"I don't care what people think of us," he confirmed.

"Good," she said, relieved to hear that.

"I do care, however, that you are fooling around with other men. If you're going to be with me, I need to know that you will be mine, and mine alone."

"Reuben, that's my past," she said swallowing her saliva in shame and regret. "When you took me on my bed that first time, that all changed. You don't have to worry about another man snaking me from you. I'm yours, and only yours. Nothing and nobody will ever come between us…I promise. You have my infinite devotion. I belong to you, Daddy, as long as you want me."

Dawn played with his hands, taking a closer look at his fingers, which had no fingernails, and whose tips actually appeared to come to a point. She gazed up at him, and looked into his deep, red eyes, and saw only perfection. Reuben's eyes were as blood red as his natural hair color. He had a slight harelip, attaching his nose to his mouth, but it was barely noticeable, especially to her. His skin was so fair and white that it was almost ghoulish in texture.

"What made you chase and assault that guy, anyway?" he asked her, dying of curiosity to know what motivated her to do such a thing.

"I was in the Mall, with some girlfriends from my cheerleading squad," she said, "A man came up, someone I never even met before, and…out of nowhere, he firmly grabbed my fanny, like he was entitled or something…like I had a fucking *welcome* sign plastered on my butt. I can't explain it. I just fucking lost it."

"You didn't seem to mind when I first got fresh with you," he commented, "and we both know I got away with doing a lot more than he did," he said grinning with accomplished pride.

"It was different with you," she said, smiling back at him.

"How?" he asked, knowing the answer all too well.

"I love you," she replied. "I've always loved you, even before we met."

"That's all I wanted to hear," he said back.

"How are you so old?" she asked, changing the subject. "You don't look like you're 41," she complimented him, being nice.

"How old do I look?" he asked her, intrigued to hear her opinion.

"I don't know," she answered. "You just look a lot younger."

"I don't know?" he said. "I don't know what I ever did, Dawn, to be so lucky to be here with you now? You are so much more than I ever could have known I wanted. You could have anybody. I don't know why you feel something for me, but I pray that I can hold on to it and keep it alive."

"I'm not going anywhere, Reuben. I'm yours, and that won't change after we're discharged. I want a life with you. I need you to hold me and never let me go."

"That won't be a problem. Just don't leave me," he begged her. Though she was his first, he knew that she would be the only one to ever want him. "Too many girls out there, say they love a man, only to later turn their back and backstab him, as if he meant nothing. I want to be a memory for you, Dawn, but I never want to be your past," Reuben stated, proving he was wise beyond his lack of experience.

"The past is the only dead thing that smells bittersweet," she said half jokingly, failing miserably at trying to lighten the mood. "I'm the one worried you're going to leave me," she confessed. "There's got to be a company out there that finds eligible people for a clinical research study, which would cater to or target people with diseases such as yours," she said, still fretting about his blood disorder potentially stealing him tragically and prematurely from her loving embrace.

Reuben tightly held her from behind, in the spooning position. She cradled his protective arms in her own, while kissing the back of his hands and sucking on the tips of his nail less fingers. Dawn wiggled and pushed her sweet ass against him, enjoying the feeling of his cock against her flawless, precious rump. As Reuben drowned in utter bliss, just holding her in his arms and laying there with the owner of his once lonely heart, he began to feel something moist soak his penis and thighs.

"What is that?" Reuben asked, feeling a warm wetness engulf and drench their bodies. "Are you peeing the bed?" he asked, surprised but strangely not disgusted.

"I'm marking my territory," she answered. "I want to make sure that every other female in heat knows who you belong to. You're taken, and I want to make that known." Though the pee kind of weirded Reuben out, how could he reasonably argue with such a sweet sentiment. She loved him back, and that was all that mattered. The smell, though unpleasant, didn't even cause him to gag. He was touched by the meaning behind it, and felt closer to her than before.

Without warning, the two had dosed off to sleep, there in the pool of piss, practically simultaneously. They had also lost complete track of the time, before slipping into their joined unconscious. There were only a couple of hours remaining, for them to safely rest, before their privacy would be invaded and their security threatened. The nurse's staff would undoubtedly be expecting to see them both at breakfast.

The little time there was left to spare, flew by like a snap of the fingers or the blink of an eye. Nurse Carl peeked in Dawn's door window, and found Reuben still spooning her, in her bed. She was laying in the fetal position, and Reuben was behind her, with his protective arm wrapped around her delectable waist and his other arm resting under her head for her to use as a pillow. They were buck naked, and keeping each other warm with their intense love for one another. Their combined body heat was all that kept them from being cold; lying in Dawn's pungent but dried urine. Reuben had fully meant to leave in plenty of time and return to his room, but they had worn each other out and the impulsive urge to stay together was simply irresistible. They had earnestly tried to stay away from each other, but after their first taste, their profound hunger for each other only grew...and grew by the moment. Besides, the risk of getting caught kind of made it hotter for both of them, though neither would ever admit to it.

Carl was one of the many male nurses who had been serviced by Dawn, but the only one among them who felt like Dawn was his personal property. He wanted Dawn for himself, and had often imagined himself ending up with her at some point down the line, though she had never given him any signals to indicate that she had felt the same. Nurse Carl had been one of the ones to give her special privileges, and let her get away with breaking the rules, in exchange for her keeping her mouth shut (that is, when it wasn't open and sealed around his shaft). He had grown increasingly frustrated since Dawn had suddenly quit meeting him at the maintenance closet, at their agreed time, for his daily head. Now, seeing them together, Carl knew why she had blown him off. Nurse Carl, in his own twisted way, was very fond of Dawn, and felt he had put in the time and effort to earn and deserve her loyal affections. Nurse Carl looked around, to make sure no one was watching, and then gently cracked opened Dawn's door, carefully and quietly shutting it behind him.

Reuben tended to sleep like a rock, and could literally sleep peacefully through a storm of the century. Dawn was much more sensitive and alert to her environment, and had a sixth sense, even when she was a bit out of it. As Carl slowly made his way to her bedside, walking as if he was stepping on eggshells, Dawn somehow heard him coming, and opened her eyes. Before Dawn could process what was about to happen, Carl had pulled Reuben off of her, and soon had him pinned on the floor. Carl held Reuben's skinny, gangly arms down, while he straddled him. Reuben's eyes were still funky, and weren't working quite yet, as they were contaminated with the morning crust and irritated redness that often plagued him.

"You had to bogart her, didn't you? Well, if I can't have her, no one will," the delusional Carl said, with unadulterated hate in his determined eyes. "Wait, is that piss I smell?" Nurse Carl asked in abhorrent and hypocritical revulsion, as he turns his head to look over at the saturated bed. "Aww, Jesus! You two are sick!"

Nurse Carl picked up Reuben's wrists and began pounding them against the hard, tiled floor, repeatedly and violently. Then, taking his right hand off Reuben's left wrist, Carl started to punch him directly in the face, over and over again. Reuben began spitting out his teeth, which were already weakened and diseases from his porphyria. Dawn yelled for Carl to stop, and show her boyfriend mercy, but it got her nowhere. She grabbed the sides of her head and shook it back and forth, as she teetered her body like a rocking chair and cried for her one true love. Seeing that Nurse Carl meant business, Dawn tried to reason with him, while tears rushed down her face, like a waterfall.

"You're right, Nurse Carl," she said with noble intent, and phony respect. "We need help. Let us see the chaplain. Maybe he can save our souls," she cried, thinking of anything she could say to try and dissuade him from hurting Reuben anymore than he already had.

"It's too late for that, luscious," he said, "You both are damned, and I'm the Grim Reaper."

Realizing that he wasn't going to dismount Reuben on his own and that she had no other alternative, Dawn courageously jumped on Nurse Carl's back, trying to get him off and away from Reuben, as she screamed desperately for help. Carl reached behind him and somehow managed to grab her by her throat, violently throwing her off of his back. Her head and body struck the wall with great force, hence knocking her out cold. She lied there, helpless and limp. Though she had bellowed loud enough for the entire minimal-security asylum to hear, no one came rushing in to investigate. Nobody cared. Nobody helped. Not a solitary soul came rushing to investigate or intervene.

Reuben saw what Nurse Carl had done to his true love, and in his battered, fatigued state, somehow found the strength and adrenaline to push Carl off of him, regardless of his injured being. Reuben, with blood clotting his eyes, brawled valiantly against Nurse Carl, but his chivalry would prove futile, and wouldn't be enough to suppress Nurse Carl's barbaric outrage. Though Reuben's vision was severely blocked and blurred from the fierce beating, and the room was now spinning on account that his sense of balance and clarity were thrown way off track, he refused to let Carl win without a fight...even if the odds were stacked against him.

"You're going to burn for what you've done," Reuben said. "You know that, don't you?"

"I'm not the one who couldn't be loved by his own blood," Nurse Carl said back. "I'm not the one who'll be forever remembered as a twisted fuck!"

"Really?" Reuben asked, "Twisted fuck? Isn't that like the pot calling the kettle black?" Reuben looked at Nurse Carl, and saw the deadly and sadistic conviction and determination is his eyes. He knew that very instant, that only one of them would survive this final battle, and walk away in one piece. "You hurt the only person who ever loved me," Reuben said, "The only person I've ever known who's worth loving."

"I don't have to take your insubordination, freak show! Your swingin' girlfriend was easy prey. If it hadn't been me, it would have been somebody else. In fact, I have it on good authority that she's shagged practically every male nurse in this ward. You're going to judge me, because of a few indiscretions, when you're sick enough to say that the world's greatest prostitute is the very epitome of love? You've got to be kidding me."

Bored and weary of wasting his breath on what he deemed to be a pathetic loser, Nurse Carl violently shoved Reuben backwards, pushing him several feet against the wall and causing him to trip over his sedated lover along the way. Nurse Carl quickly pulled out his electric shock baton from its sheath, which hung off of his utility belt.

"Come on!" Nurse Carl challenged in a hostile manner and threatening tone. "I'm calling you out! Let's see what you've got, Reuben Ian Peterson!"

Just as Reuben gallantly and dauntlessly lunged to strike back, Nurse Carl abruptly and aggressively speared him in the heart with his savage weapon, so ruthlessly that the baton broke off in his chest...thereby forever breaking Dawn's heart as well. Nurse Carl then mounted the fallen hero, seized Reuben by the head, and using both hands, resumed bashing his head against the floor violently and repeatedly, until the back of Reuben's head cracked open like a fresh head of iceberg lettuce, or an overly ripe melon. He then proceeded to take his thumbs and poke out Reuben's red eyes, like he was crudely carving a seasonal jack o' lantern.

When the frenzied Dawn came to, Nurse Carl had cowardly split the scene, leaving her alone with the limp corpse of her bloodied and optically dismembered beloved. She sat there frozen in shock, staring at her butchered suitor, the one who had given her reason to live and the ability to love. Sitting with her legs bent, and her arms hugging just below her knees, she wept silently but frantically. Still, not a soul had come rushing in to check out the bedlam of commotion. She manically rocks back and forth, as she can feel her mind permanently snapping. She reaches down with her left hand and rubs her intricate, tribal dream catcher ankle tattoo, as if turning to her spiritual, native roots one last time for guidance. The ancient ghosts of her ancestors ignored her, much in the way that God had forsaken her and Reuben, and the last bit of humanity she carried inside of her had dissolved and disappeared.

Reuben had hastily become everything to her, and had now been taken as rapidly as he was given. Tears rushed and washed down her grieving face, as she now knelt in her nakedness, as if praying to the God who had so clearly turned his back. Despite the sanctified appearance, she wasn't calling out to God, but rather renouncing him. Goosebumps and cold chills covered her exposed and raving body, as she literally trembled in unbearable pain and indescribable anger. Her jaw was having involuntary tremors, and she couldn't get her unstable hands to stop shaking on their own.

Dawn brought her delicate hands up in front of her face, and watched in horror as her fingernails suddenly and graphically transformed into long, razor sharp claws. She didn't know if this was an illusion brought on by rage, or if it was really happening...and she honestly didn't care. She also felt every single one of her teeth grow into ferocious fangs. Again, she couldn't decipher what was real, and what wasn't. All she knew was that her soulmate had been brutally butchered, and she was going to make them pay. Digging her hand into Reuben's open wound, she covered and coated her hand in his blood, then brought it up top her mouth and sucked it off her fingers, feeling that it was a way to keep him in her forever, even though he was gone. She looked up at the door behind her destroyed and demolished boyfriend, and instinctively knew what she had to do. As retribution fueled her adrenalin, the furious and nude Dawn jumped to her feet, and leapt toward the door like a rabid panther. Dawn would release a wrath of biblical proportions that even the celestial Almighty himself couldn't match.

Gradually stepping out of her room, Dawn heard the song *Eve of Destruction*, by Barry McGuire, playing. Nurse Carl had put it on, and was playing it over the intercom, as if either to be deliberately boastful or unknowingly prophetic. She began walking leisurely and eerily towards the nurse's station. As she did, staff and patient alike stopped dead in their tracks, and stared at her in both amazement and repulsion. A couple of people even keeled over and vomited on the floor, after seeing her shaggy, unclad self. Dawn pinpointed Nurse Carl, who was standing behind the counter, casually going through paperwork, as if nothing had happened and it was business as usual. He didn't even raise an eyebrow to acknowledge her, as she serenely approached the desk.

"You need to go back to your room," one of the female RNs ordered, while fighting not to puke at the sight of her.

Dawn, not dignifying her edict with a response, focused on keeping her eye on the bigger fish. Effortlessly leaping over the crescent-shaped counter top, as if she had suddenly become an accomplished Olympic gymnast, she now stood merely inches away from Nurse Carl. People around them continued to goggle, remain still, and just spectate in unadulterated disbelief. Nurse Carl strangely couldn't see the claws or the fangs, but he did see the fatal look of certain death in Dawn's vengeful eyes.

"Are you scared?" she asked Nurse Carl. "If not, you should be."

Nurse Carl started to speak, but before he could have the chance, Dawn grabbed him and pushed him up against the wall, knocking several things onto the floor, such as a *Playboy* Playmate calendar and a Lux Smiley Face *Have A Happy Day* yellow, electric wall clock. Dawn had used such blunt force, that Carl's fat back had made a body-shaped crack in the wall. The other nurses on duty hung their mouths open in dreadful awe, as they watched Dawn rise up Carl, who hefted at least twice her own weight, and held him with one hand, nearly a foot off the ground.

"What do you want?" Nurse Carl asked, noticing that nobody had the balls to restrain or sedate her, and that he was clearly on his own.

"I want a confession," she said.

"Confession to what?" he asked, standing his ground, and sticking to his fabricated alibi that he had premeditated in his warped, self-absorbed head.

"It's okay," Dawn said. "I lied. I don't need a confession."

"So, you'll let me down then?" he asked, relieved that she had come to reason.

"Let you down? But I thought you liked being up?" she said, as she used her free hand to stick down the front of his pants. She began playing with his sweaty testicles, cupping them in her soft hand, as the frightened Carl began to get sexually aroused, even in this immediate realm of imminent danger.

"Hey," Nurse Carl added, "You know what they say, right? Absence makes the mind grow fonder. They also say you don't know what you got till it's gone, but…I think we both know that you didn't lose much. Reuben wasn't worth your time. He wasn't good enough for you. He didn't have what we both know you need."

Just as Nurse Carl began to moan in jubilant pleasure and conveniently forget about her deranged mental state, Dawn tightened her grip on his filthy scrotum and ripped it clear off of his bloated body, causing his covetous groin to spew and gush blood all over the front of his pants. Everyone who witnessed this began to scream in terror, and run for their very lives. The psyche facility had become a den of chaos and it was everyone for themselves. Nobody had any intention on trying to exact revenge for Nurse Carl's murder, nor had any interest in getting anywhere near enough to Dawn to foolishly attempt to subdue her rage. Everyone on staff knew Carl to be a despicable scumbag, and neither his execution nor their salaries were worth risking their own lives. Dawn was clearly on a death mission of dire determination, and no one wished to stand in her way.

"I want my boyfriend back, you son of a bitch!" Dawn said, as she pulled out his severed nuts from the front of his pants and shoved them into his mouth, pushing them down his throat, as he gagged in futile resistance. Dropping him on the floor, Nurse Carl twitched and convulsed dramatically, as he choked on his own balls, until he finally quit breathing and his cold heart finally stopped. Dawn looked down one last time at Carl, whose blood still flowed through and out of his pant legs, and continued to make a vast pool around him of both blood and urine. She spit on him, as her way of giving herself closure to what he had so unjustly purloined from her.

"Goodnight, john-boy," she said, to the damaged Vietnam Vet.

One of the other scared nurses responsibly activated the clamorous alarm, initiating a containment lockdown. This was Dawn's cue to get fully engrossed in her honorable endeavor of justified vengeance, while she still had the opportunity, freedom and the time to do so. Dawn lashed out in total retribution, mutilating and exterminating everyone in the facility, in brutal dismemberment. She ran around on her bare knuckles, much like the primitive characters in the acclaimed *Planet of the Apes* movie, savagely and barbarically tearing people limb from limb, methodically and one at a time.

Dawn finally found herself in an overdue confrontation with the tyrannical Dr. Aaron, that was a long time coming.

"Dawn," Dr. Aaron said, "You don't want to do this. Don't let your hatred define you, or you will become what you despise the most," secretly referring to himself, figuring that she was coming after him in a personal vendetta, for being one of the ones to take advantage of her sexual vulnerability. "Remember what we've discussed in my office," he continued in vane to attempt to reason with her. "Hurt people hurt people. Don't become one of those people."

"If that's your way of calling me a monster," she said, "just remember...you made me."

"Stop!" Dr. Aaron said, trying one last time to get through to her, "Your anger is misdirected! You and I both know that you really want to kill your father, not me," he stressed, trying desperately to effectively remove the blame from himself and get her to add his contributed share to the pedophile crimes of her clergyman father. "You're taking your anger out on me! Don't do that! You're out of control! If you kill me, you risk reverting back to the drawing board and losing all the progress you have made here with us!"

"I know what my father is, and I know what you are," she replied, "and I've never been more in control."

"You're a sorry slut, Dawn," Dr. Aaron said boldly, now accepting that he wasn't going to get out of this alive, or at least not on two legs, "I always thought you were a lousy hussy."

"That's funny, I never heard you complain," Dawn said, after snickering at his conceited nerve.

"Come on!" he tempted her, "If you're going to do something, go ahead and do it! Don't just stand there like a pathetic trollop, you fucking waste of flesh!" he provoked her. "You fucking tease! You Lolita floozy!"

Dawn sneered at him in disgust, before jumping high into the air and landing in a scissor lock, with her inner thighs wrapped around his pretentious neck. As he began to lose his balance, with her crotch literally in his face, she twisted her hips and snapped his neck. Dr. Aaron fell straight backwards, with Dawn still straddling his face, while she firmly held the top of his head like it was the halter of a saddle bronc horse. Grasping his hair with her left hand, she threw her right arm up and behind her, while howling in victory, like some deranged werewolf cowgirl. When they settled, she landed safely on her feet, and the back of his head collided and cracked with the hard floor, with her help of course.

Dawn immediately resorted and resumed to stalking her next prey, as the ward was in an intense state of panic and hysteria, as staff and patient alike ran around like headless chickens. Dawn targeted and attacked everyone, one after the other, whimsically and unsystematically as though her appetite was insatiable and her thirst for ferocious retaliation was unquenchable. Slaughtering these people left and right brought her a sense of contentment that was refreshingly emancipating. Then, to her appeased gratification, she spotted the obese and offensive Kenneth.

"Damn, girl," Kenneth said, "I always knew you were a circus freak, but I had no idea just how much," he said daringly, somehow arrogantly confident that she had no power over him, and that she lacked the strength to conquer him.

The doughty Dawn equably walked up to approach and engage with Kenneth, bare-naked and drenched in blood.

"Kenneth," she said. "You have just what I need."

"Damn girl," he said again, proud of himself and happy to hear her boost his already inflated ego. "I thought you'd never come around," he said with an obnoxious smile, as he began unzipping his strangulating pants, reaching under his grossly stout belly.

"That wasn't exactly what I had in mind," she said teasing him, as she seductively closed in on him, where he anxiously stood waiting to see what she had to offer. "I was thinking more along the lines of something you could actually see...not something that's totally out of sight." Before he had a moment to identify her deception, Dawn punched a hole through Kenneth's gluttonous stomach, and began yanking out his lower intestines, like she was a magician pulling tied handkerchiefs out of a trick top hat.

While Kenneth spit out a heinous concoction of his vile blood and upchuck, Dawn turned around and used his intestines to rope Nurse Claire who was foolishly trying to make a belated run for it. Lassoing the intestines around the pitiless nurse's neck, she tugged the human lariat, and literally swept Nurse Claire off her enlarged feet, bringing her to thwack the back of her head on the rigid, tiled floor. Dawn dragged the stocky nurse toward her, so that she could have better access to her corpulent body.

"It's morning time, Nurse Claire," Dawn announced, "and you haven't made the rounds yet. Slacking again on the job, I see. Don't you want to dispense your favorite mystery pill?" Dawn gave the intestines one last hard heave, and snapped Claire's neck like a brittle twig. "Guess you finally had a taste of your own medicine, huh?" she said to the portly corpse.

The feral Dawn killed indiscriminately, not aiming for just the ones who deserved it, but demolishing everyone in her path. She had broken not only mentally, but also in every aspect and on every level. Mankind had incurred her indomitable wrath, and it was not going to subside until the earth became her personal slaughterhouse. The other patients, whom she had gotten to know so well, and even befriended in some cases, all begged her for exemption, but she showed no mercy. Dawn tore through her peers as cutthroat and as effortlessly as she did her shameless tormenters.

Walking into different rooms to ensure that no stone was left unturned, Dawn stumbled upon Barbara, who was still catatonic and had since been placed in a straight jacket, as if she had posed some kind of threat to others, by not being able to move or function. Barbara was sitting on her lower bunk, just staring off into space, as if trapped in a looped nightmare which she had no route of escape. Dawn looked at her in sincere commiseration, before ruthlessly tearing her throat out with her bare hands, and throwing the bloody contents on the floor.

"I'm deeply sorry, Barbara," she said, as the lobotomized woman toppled over to the floor, face first, "but I'm sure you're probably better off this way," she said, considering this more or less of a mercy killing. "My condolences."

The blaring alarm continued to annoy and deafen, but Dawn unremittingly stayed the course, butchering the few remaining victims who were misfortunate enough to be left occupying or wandering the loony bin.

Nurse Gregory hurriedly came running around the corner, and saw Dawn, completely immersed in the blood of those lives she had taken.

"Dawn?" he called out to her. "What are you doing? This is crazy! Stop! Just stop!" he tried with futile effort to rationalize with her fury.

"Nurse Gregory," she said softly, "You were the only male nurse in this ward who didn't screw me in one way or another," she said. "I just wanted you to know that I truly appreciate that."

"So, we're copacetic then?" he asked her, relieved to hear her say that she hadn't taken his kindness for granted. "You'll let me cut out?"

"You'll leave here, alright," she replied, "but only in a doggie bag."

"I thought you said we were cool?" he said, backing up from her, as she slowly and calmly walked toward him.

"We are," she confirmed, "but, I can't have any witnesses."

"Please," he pleaded again, for her thoughtful consideration to let him be the exception.

"No way, Jose," she replied.

"Dawn!" William said from behind her. "What are you doing? You have to stop this! Please!"

Dawn turned around, looking like Sissy Spacek at the end of *Carrie*, and faced her self-righteous friend. "William...another male resident here, who never tried to get a piece of this tail" she said, as she patted and rubbed her ass with both hands. "You better look away. Scripture tells us that if you even look at a woman out of lust, you are sinning against God," she quoted, as William swallowed his saliva and his pride, not wanting to own up to his own infatuation of Dawn. "What's wrong, William? I'm not good enough for you to Bible thump...or I should say, hump?"

"Dawn...listen...you can talk to me. I'm your friend. Jesus loves you, and so do I. Let me be here for you. Please."

"Your Jesus never loved me, William. God only blesses the callous and the cruel, and pisses on the pure of heart. That's the God you serve, whether you see it that way or not. God forsook me a long time ago, and stonewalled me when I asked him why, much like he did to his own son. God took away the only man who ever really loved me, as quickly as he gave him to me. God's nothing but an Indian giver; that's the God of the Bible, William, not the figment of fantasy you make him out to be."

"The Lord is close to the brokenhearted," William said in response, not sure what else to say.

"AAHH!!" Dawn screamed, as she leapt towards William and slashed his face with her razor-sharp talons, in the formation of the Sign of the Cross, forever marking him the way that God had historically marked Cain. "What the fuck does your God think I am?!"

As Dawn was butchering William, Nurse Gregory used that as an opportunity to cut loose. Scared shitless, Nurse Gregory was actually able to reach the exit, and escape with his life in tact, while Dawn was preoccupied with her distraction. Though Dawn had logical reason to be concerned about leaving witnesses, Gregory had no intention of ever telling a soul about her or what she had done. He was just grateful to be alive, and to survive such an atrocious genocide.

When Dawn was finished massacring whom she could lay her hands on, she walked into the same shower stall that she had earlier shared with Reuben. When she got there, she found Nurse Monica cringing and hiding in the shower. Dawn just stood there over her, as Monica shook like a leaf in a whirlwind.

"Why didn't you come see what was wrong, when I screamed for someone to help Reuben?" Dawn asked her. "Why? Why didn't you come? I know you heard me. Did you think I was just crying wolf? You were the one nurse in this hellhole that I actually thought gave a shit."

"That's not true," Nurse Monica refuted. "Nurse Gregory cared about you and Reuben too. He cared about all of you, like I do. I'm sorry, Dawn. I would have come running, to help Reuben. I didn't know anything had happened. I just came on shift a little while ago. I was late getting to work today. If I had been here, I would have helped you. Forgive me. I'm so sorry."

Dawn just stared at Nurse Monica for several minutes, huffing and puffing, while contemplating whether or not to blow her life away too. As Monica wept and pleaded for her life, Dawn could see in her eyes that she wasn't playing mind games with her, but that she did actually care.

"If I let you go," Dawn began, "Do you give me your solemn word that you won't speak a peep about this, or about me, to anyone?"

"Yes," Monica replied, as her rapid heart rate began to calm, suddenly seeing the look of compassion in Dawn's eyes. "I swear, Dawn, I will never tell a soul."

"Okay," Dawn reluctantly but sympathetically agreed. "You can leave. I won't harm you. You're free to go, Monica. Thanks for caring about Reuben and I. We appreciate your friendship."

"Oh…thank you, Dawn. Thank you. Thank you for my life," Nurse Monica profusely expressed her gratitude. "Again, I'm sorry for everything that happened to both of you."

"Let me help you up, Monica." Dawn reached out her arm, and though Monica was hesitant at first to take her hand, she trusted her in spite of the macabre circumstances.

As Monica ran out of the communal restroom and bath area, she took off down the hall like a bat out of Hell. Dawn calmly stepped into the shower stall, treating it like a decontamination chamber, and washed the majority of the blood off of her young body, which was amazingly relaxed and not trembling. Getting out of the shower, she wiped the tears from her blue eyes, and in a way, said her reluctant goodbyes to the fond, but too few, memories she had shared with Reuben.

Just when she thought she was alone in the ward, she saw Joshua running, but he wasn't trying to make a zippy break for the exit. Joshua, instead, was witlessly running towards her. When he got close enough to do so, Joshua stopped dead in his tracks in front of her, and slapped her hard in the face, with his limp wrist. Dawn looked at him, and saw that he was smiling, as if anxiously anticipating his punishment for assaulting her. As if reading her mind, Joshua turned around, so that his back faced her.

"God forgives," Joshua told her, as if to relieve her from any guilt or fault, for what she was about to do to him.

"I'm not God," Dawn replied. "God kills indiscriminately, and now so do I."

Dawn grabbed him in a headlock, and quickly snapped his neck. Dawn felt Joshua deserved a better send off than this, but didn't want to get any more blood on her, now that she had just bathed. She dragged him over to the nurse's station, and picked him up to lay him back first on the counter, as if it were suddenly an altar. She then walked over to the record player, and found the album *The Crazy World of Arthur Brown*. She placed the record on the turntable, and played the song *Fire*, while she went to her room and retrieved her silver flask. Pouring the last of her Moonshine over Joshua's body, she used a book of matches to ignite the saturated corpse, and then walked away, as if leaving a campfire.

She searched the premises and eventually tracked down where the alarm was coming from. Breaking the security system, simply by ripping out the wires and utterly dismantling and disassembling the sheer mechanics of it, she managed to both overturn the alarm and unlock the hellish facility.

"Let's blow this taco stand," she said, as if talking to Reuben's immortal ghost.

Coming down from her frantic condition, Dawn casually walked out of the ward, leaving the doors and gates wide open, making it easy for anyone else to duck out, if she had mistakenly left anyone there alive.

By the time clinic security got around to barging in, from the main infirmary upstairs, everyone in the destroyed mental health facility was declared and pronounced dead. Little did the local smokeys know that one particular female RN had been stripped of her property. Monica had fled with Dawn's permission and blessing, but in her rush to vacate the scene; Monica had dropped her identity badge and keys. Dawn had noticed this and picked the useful items off the floor, just a few feet from the communal shower room. Dawn had also paid a visit to the employee lounge, and taken Nurse Monica's purse and casual threads from her locker. Because the annihilation was already in progress when Monica had reported late to work, she was immediately flustered with fear and temporarily forgot that she had just put her essentials in her locker. Because Dawn had petrified her with debilitating terror as she ran off, Monica never made it back to her locker to grab her belongings. The boob tube in the solarium is cranked up to the maximum volume, and the band Starbuck is performing their hit song *Moonlight Feel Right* on a televised recap from the previous week's variety show, *The Midnight Special*.

Meanwhile, Dawn had hastily retreated to the woods, like a fox on the run. She's garbed in the stolen nurse's pink and white *Doors* baseball jersey; brown suede *Winlit* shearling Boho ladies coat; faded blue, hip-hugger bellbottom jeans; and brand new clogs, and still has a bit of nearly-dried blood in her hair, that failed to come out in the shower. She finds a creek, and climbs down the rocky surface to get closer to the water. Carefully kneeling down by the stream, she uses her hands to wash the rest of the blood out of her long, brown hair. The water is bitterly ice-cold, but she does it anyway. She knows that it's only a matter of time before the fuzz put it together, when they learn that she is the only patient unaccounted for. As she's rinsing the last of the blood out of her hair, she sees Reuben's reflection in the ripples. His face is clear as crystal, but only for a brief, fleeting moment. As his short-lived image dissipates into nothingness, she hears his doting voice in her head as she continues to gaze into the water.

"I will never truly die, unless you forget me," the voice says.

Dawn looks up, and sees a wolf standing across from her, on the other side of the creek. This wasn't a mirage or a reflection, but what appeared to be an actual, physical timber wolf. It was beautiful, and magnificent, with fur that was various shades of grey, white, black, and rusty brown, with piercing yellow eyes. Wolves weren't typically native to Virginia, so this was unexpected naturally, as well as supernaturally. The wolf was carrying a human baby between its teeth. The baby was alive and unharmed, but had red eyes, and a face that resembled her lost love. She had Native American relatives on her father's side, but had never experienced a mystical vision or been on a spirit quest. She didn't know if that was what she was seeing, or if what she was seeing was the real deal...or perhaps it was something somewhere in between. Either way, the wolf in front of her appeared non-threatening, and even affable. But, as she reached out her hand to entice it closer, the wolf and the infant, like Reuben's reflection, vanished before her sorrowful eyes.

"See you on the flip side, Daddy," she said softly, saying her final farewell to her deceased lover.

JULY 9, 1959

The pitch sky was particularly dark and misty that night. The full moon emanated an eerie glow, which seemed to celebrate the figurative fire brewing in the Maryland middle-class suburb beneath it. This house could have easily been compared to the Cleaver home in the *Leave it to Beaver* television show, with one distinct exception. There was no aggression or hostility in the Cleaver residence.

Richard and Shirley sat at their dinner table, with their disgrace of a daughter seated directly across from them. The rubber tree plant sat in the corner of the tacky, lemon pattern wallpapered kitchen. Linda was only 17, and getting ready to have her baby out of wedlock. 1959 was a retro period in America where tradition was still everything, and casual sex was actually frowned upon. Love was an unacceptable excuse, because even if loyalty was an element in the relationship, if it was premarital, it was wrong; no exceptions. Linda had done something unforgivable, at least in her parents' eyes, for being knocked up and not first being married. As if that wasn't embarrassing enough, the fact that she had chosen to sleep with a tribal Indian, was miles beyond what her parents could or would handle.

"Have you considered giving it up for adoption yet?" Shirley asked, in the calmest voice that she could manage to speak.

"It's not an *it*, Mom," Linda replied in disgusted disparage and defamation.

"Don't you dare disrespect your mother at my table!" her belligerent father bellowed out, glaring at her with a somber stare.

"Oh, so I can disrespect her away from the table?" Linda asked her impertinent question in flagrant sarcasm and derision.

You could almost see the hot steam come out of Dick's ears. "It's not her fault that she had a whore!" he said. "I'm not to blame either for my daughter having a bastard!"

"Honey," the deferential Shirley whispered, with her courteous head bowed and her eyes focused on her partially empty plate. "Please try not to raise your voice." The well-trained wife rubbed her feet together like a nervous cricket, wearing her favorite Satin Slippers that were the same shade of red as her dominant husband's cotton slacks.

"Bastard?" Linda said back. "Seriously, Dad? What a horrible word to use about your grandchild. How can you speak that way about my baby?" she asked, now in tears.

"Sweetheart, we just don't understand," her crestfallen mother replied on her angry husband's behalf. "This was not how we brought you up. You were raised to honor the written Word of God, and to respect the sacred institution of marriage."

"Mom," Linda said. "No offense, but there is nothing sacred about marriage. Look at what it's done for you. You and Dad don't even sleep in the same bed anymore. You have separate rooms. Besides, I've encountered kids at school, whose parents are getting divorced, just because one of them has lost interest in the other or was caught cheating. Marriage has become a joke, and I want no part of that."

"Now that's quite enough!" Richard screamed. "I will not have this insolence in my house! I am an American soldier, goddammit! I deserve your respect!"

"You weren't even good enough to go to Vietnam," Linda said spontaneously without thinking about the consequences.

Her father got real quiet and paused for several minutes, while his face blushed with shame and chagrin. "I was supposed to go," he said in a hushed tone. "I couldn't, because of my injury. You know that. Would you have rather seen me gone and be killed in combat? Is that what you want? Is that what you're trying to do? Kill me? Kill your father?"

"Baby," Shirley began again, still making every effort to speak gently and meekly. "He's not even white."

"I fought at Pearl Harbor," Richard muttered under his heavy breath. "But I suppose that means nothing to a spoiled cunt like my own sperm."

"Mom," Linda responded with a dirty look while disregarding her father's crude slander, "he's a minister."

"Are you planning on marrying this boy?" her mother said, still in denial that he was considerably older than Linda and doing her best to push the brainwashing seed of marriage, hoping to get her wayward daughter to give in and comply. "Are you even committed to him? Can you be faithful? Are you planning on staying with him?"

"Of course I'm committed," the licentious Linda lied through her cum-washed teeth. "Why would I hurt him? I love him. He's the man of my dreams."

"Then why are you putting us through this nightmare?" her indignant father asked, as tactfully as he could, while subconsciously grinding his teeth and clinching his cloth napkin in his fists under the table. "He's good enough to fuck, but not marry? Is that it?" he added, while struggling to maintain a sensitive and non-threatening volume.

"Are you trying to get me to runaway?" Linda asked her parents. "Would you both prefer that? Would that make you happy, to see your daughter and grandchild alone and lost?"

"I'm sure you have places you could go," her father bluntly remarked. "Your mother and I have overheard your phone calls. We see how you're dressed when you come home from school. A different boy picks you up every other week. You're seventeen and pregnant, for God's sake. If Mingan won't take you in, I'm sure you could easily shack up with one of your other regulars," he spoke to her, as if she were a common prostitute.

"Well, fine then," Linda said back, while her chin quivered. "If that's the way you feel, I'll go and I won't ever come back."

"Go ahead," her father invited. "I dare you. I don't expect you'll get too far though. I doubt you have a quarter for a gallon of gas. Oh wait, I forgot, you don't even own a car. Yeah, that's right, you're seventeen and still my dependent. I know you're not considering stealing mine. You touch my *Crown Victoria*, and you'll regret it," he warned her, very proud and protective of his pink and white 1955 *Ford*.

"Dad," she said, this time using a tone that was more proper and less curt, "I don't understand why we necessarily have to be married in order to be a family?"

"Because that's how it's done!" he immediately answered her, once again losing control of his already ill temper. "That's how things are done, Linda! You're born, you go to school, you go to college, you get a job, you get married, and then you have babies! That's the right order to live your life! Any other way is inappropriate and intolerable!"

"Your father's right, honey," Shirley contributed, once again being humble and subservient. "You're only seventeen. This bastard will ruin your life. What will your baby's last name be, if you're not legally married to the father? Bane or Moon? Have you thought about that?"

"You know," Linda said chuckling and shaking her head, "I am getting really fucking tired of you both referring to my unborn baby as a bastard."

Richard tugged on his cream-colored *Jockey* undershirt, and pondered the idea of disowning his only daughter, and putting her out into the streets where he felt she belonged anyway. The only thing that kept him from acting on this callous temptation was the prospect of his grandchild. Though he didn't approve of how he would be a grandfather, there was a hidden part of him buried deep down, which yearned to know his unborn grandchild. Richard made eye contact with his loose daughter, as he drooled his toxic saliva like a mad dog.

"The USSR is beating us in our race to the moon," Richard said, after letting out one last sigh of contempt. "If you're not careful, I'm going to beat you," he told his pregnant daughter, without hesitation or second thought.

This hypocritical habitation was as vain as they were Bane. Richard had the country's updated flag waving from a planted iron pole, in the front yard, to illustrate their pride for Dick having been in the US military. All forty-nine stars waved back and forth, on windy days, as if to brag to the neighborhood of Mr. Bane's bigoted patriotism.

NOVEMBER 20, 1968

Dawn stared at the lime green, rotary dial telephone that sat on the two tier end table, while she lounged on the orange *Henredon* curved sofa. She felt subdued, as she had been coerced into temporarily staying at the next-door neighbor's, while waiting for her mother to get out of jail.

Linda had been arrested for leading and organizing a Vietnam War protest in DC. She had packed some friends in a graffiti decorated 1963 Volkswagen bus, and shuttled off to the nation's capital. They gathered at Dupont Circle, and planned to march to Pennsylvania Ave and have a nonviolent sit-in. Officials told them that they were obstructing a state highway, and were threatened with police intervention. Nevertheless, the protesters marched down Main Street and stopped traffic. Once they reached the White House, they all sat in a circle and chained themselves together. When the police arrived at the scene, the local authorities and civil defense squad surrounded Linda and her fellow hippies. The peaceful protestors were mercilessly beaten with nightsticks until they finally handed over the key to unlock their heavy chains and railroad ties they had brought with them.

Dawn sat impatiently in silence, while the slutty teenage daughter hosted a party in her neglectful parents' absence, right there in the living room. Dawn went ignored, as the co-ed students played naughty games of *Twister* on the floor, raided the off-limits liquor cabinet, and made out with each other, while they groped and danced to the LP songs of popular bands like *Creedence Clearwater Revival* and *Steppenwolf*.

After hours of nobody noticing Dawn's presence, Allison finally acknowledged the little girl. Dawn was crying, softly but heavily. The irresponsible and inebriated host plopped down beside her young houseguest, and inquired about her reasons for being so sullen and disconsolate.

"What's the matter, baby girl?" Allison asked, with her eyes barely able to stay open. "Are you okay?" she asked the scared Grade-schooler, pretending to care.

"I want my Mommy," Dawn said, feeling isolated and frightened without her mother.

"Honey, your Mommy is behind bars, and your Daddy is off in Haiti or some shit, doing missionary work," Allison reminded her. "You'll be okay. We'll take care of you," she promised Dawn, as if authentically concerned, yet clearly insensitive.

After several minutes, Allison eventually began to recognize Dawn's critical state. Dawn was legitimately terrified and worried about her absent mother. Allison, though not clearheaded, stepped up to the plate and took this matter seriously, for Dawn's sake.

"Your grandparents never understood about your mother being a free spirit," she told Dawn. "They told her that you being born would ruin her life. They were wrong. You *are* her life."

Dawn looked up at Allison, as if to say with her eyes that she doubted what she was saying, though simultaneously and desperately needing to believe that she somehow knew what she was talking about.

"Your Mommy talks to my Mom, Dawn. They're friends. My Mom tells me things that your Mommy says, when she and I spend quality time. Linda adores you, sweetie. You must know that."

Dawn cracked a partial smile, while tears continued to stream and roll down her young cheeks.

"I know it hurts, baby," she said to the nine-year-old. "Your Mommy will be back. Yeah, she's in jail right now, but she won't be for very long. She's just guilty of protesting. It's not like she's some hardcore criminal or mass murderer. They won't be able to detain her for much longer. You'll see, she'll be home before you know it," she told Dawn, nudging her shoulder with her own, trying to cheer her up and lift her spirits. "Do you like any boys at school?" She asked Dawn, desperately trying to change the subject and get her mind off her activist mother. "What grade are you in now? Fourth?"

"Yeah," Dawn said softly, while she shrugged her shoulders.

"Well, tell me," Allison imposed on her privacy. "What's his name?"

"Jeffrey," Dawn answered, while keeping her head bowed to hide the flow of her tears.

"Well, does he live around here?" Allison intruded again. "Maybe I can have someone go pick him up and bring him over here, if his parents give me permission? Would you like that? So you could have somebody to play with, while I socialize with my friends?"

"He's moving away," Dawn confided.

"Oh. I'm sorry. Well, I'm sure he's going to miss you. How could he not miss a cute little girl like you? He must be heartbroken."

"No," Dawn corrected her. "He told me after school, yesterday, that he was happy to be rid of me. He never really cared about me at all."

"Oh, baby, I'm so sorry," Allison sympathized. "Unfortunately, you're learning this now, at such a fragile age. I want you to listen to me, honey, and remember what I tell you today. Boys are scum. They're all jerks. All they want us for is our bodies, and then they throw us away like we're trash. I'm sorry that you're feeling this way, Dawn. You have a tender heart and I'm very sad to see it butchered, but time will heal your wounds. Trust me. It will get easier to blow it off and let go. That's probably the most important advice I can give you as a woman. You need to learn to let go of the people who leave you. They don't care about you, so you shouldn't care about them. Trust me, they're not worth it."

"If that's true, then why did Mommy marry Daddy?" Dawn asked, showing even then that she was special and perceptive. "If you feel that way, why do you have boys at your party? Why not just girls?"

"Your Daddy is different. He's a good man. He loves your Mommy, and he loves you. Your grandparents condemned your parents' romance, because of the shade of his skin, which was terribly wrong. It was also hypocritical to show your Daddy such extreme prejudice, since your Daddy is what they call a Native American. From what I hear, your grandparents are smug Americans. So, your Daddy should have been someone they found easy to embrace, rather than quick to reject."

Just then, the power went out, without a hint of warning. The record scratched on the subsequently affected player and the lights in the house went completely dark. Nobody could see the person in front of them, as it was well after nightfall. Once the sun had gone down that evening, the rain began to pour as if it would be Heaven's last chance at storming wrath upon the earth. Once the electricity had failed, raging balls of hail began to loudly hit the roof above them, which only added to Dawn's delicate condition.

"AAHH!" Dawn screamed in horror. "Mommy!"

This power outage quickly sobered up Allison, as she instinctively wrapped her protective arms around Dawn, with the intention of offering the little girl some solace and compassion. Dawn covered her eyes with her open hands, to avoid seeing what she couldn't see.

"I'm scared, Allison!" Dawn said. "I'm scared of the darkness!"

OCTOBER 31, 1977

Dawn knew that she would eventually be caught, and when that time came, she would either feel the end of a hot bullet, or face several consecutive lifetimes in prison. There was no turning back, as she had far surpassed the point of no return and took that final plunge of faith off the apex of Mount Everest. She had sealed her fateful destiny back at the ward. She decided that if she couldn't get people to listen to the truth, she was going to take as many people down with her as possible. The refreshed Dawn had left the final trace of her sanity at the mental facility. She left the flowing creek, and climbed back up to the main road. Sticking her thumb out, she resorted to hitchhiking, beginning her new life as a crazed psychopath, as she heard the song *Crazy On You*, by Heart, playing exclusively and privately in her head.

As she walked by the side of the highway, a multitude of motor vehicles passed her by, even flicked her off, until finally, an emerald green 1972 Chevrolet *Townsman* Station Wagon pulled over. Before Dawn knew it, she was sitting in the back seat, in between two small, grade-school-aged children. The man driving was turning the dial on the car stereo, and just happened to stop on a radio station that was halfway through playing the same hit song, by the rock band *Heart*, that had just been stuck in her head. Dawn smiled, at the amusing coincidence. It was as if some mystical force was telling her that she was meant to get into this unsuspecting family automobile.

"I'm Starfire," the driver introduced himself, "and this is my funky Yin, Moonbeam," he said, referring to the woman who was riding shotgun.

"I suppose you could call me Wolfsbane," Dawn said, keeping with their psychedelic mood.

"Wicked," he said, approving of her hip name.

"Nice to meet you," Moonbeam said, "Those are our kids, Meadow and Garcia."

"Where you headed?" the mother asked.

"West," Dawn said. "I'd appreciate it, however far you can take me."

"Sure thing," the father said. "We're happy to oblige. We believe in karma, so we try to give whenever we can."

"Dig it," Moonbeam said, "Just don't expect to get there fast. We're taking a slow ride," she stated, acting as if she were doped up on some kind of mood-altering substance.

The parents were dressed like unbathed flower children. The man had the tie-dye buttoned down shirt and bandanna, and the woman wore a gypsy gown, with a light brown suede fringe jacket draped over it.

The father even had the heavy sideburns, long greasy hair, beaded necklace, circular eyeglass frames, and the bleached jean jacket with the oversized, floppy collar. The kids had bellbottoms on. The son wore a Pink Floyd *The Dark Side of the Moon* Tour T-shirt, and the daughter wore a solid pink T-shirt with a *John Travolta* Iron-On heat transfer in the center. There were still plenty hippies left, who continued to strive to keep the Movement alive, and Dawn just happened to be fortunate enough to encounter some on her getaway.

"Well," Dawn paused, "I appreciate you stopping," Dawn repeated, not sure what else to say to the psychedelic couple.

The boy and girl, both of whom looked to be in the 6-7 range, were obnoxiously loud and carrying on. They were screaming in a high-pitched squeal and seemed to deliberately misbehave, with no regard whatsoever to Dawn being there. The kids were yelling profusely about wanting to go trick or treating, even though it was far from being close to sundown. The impatient, undisciplined kids weren't buckled up, or had unhooked themselves, but either way; the parents seemed more than unconcerned. The unwed couple in the front seat never took notice, or if they did, never bothered to say a word to their rowdy, unhinged children. Dawn kept getting smacked in the face by both kids, not being able to differentiate if the young siblings were quarreling or just being nauseatingly awful. Then, before Dawn knew what she had done, the little boy had taken out his chewed stick of *Bub's Daddy* brand gum, and handed it to his sister, who then proceeded to stick it in Dawn's hair.

"I feel wired," Moonbeam said, bouncing up and down in her seat, like an overly hyperactive child on a sugar rush, "Let's find a music festival somewhere. I think someone told me there's a major gig happening in California somewhere, sometime this week."

"Right on," he agreed, "California dreaming all the way, baby!" Starfire looked in his rear view mirror, and admired how tasty Dawn looked, "Speaking of all the way, you look like a far out chick, who knows where it's at" the father harassed with ease, "Would you maybe be interested in jelling with us for a while?"

Dawn had to lean in, and cuff her open hands around the outside of her ears, just to strain to hear what the couple was saying to her.

"We're kind of on a trip," the wife added, "Don't really have a destination yet, just seeing God's green country. We'd love to have you accompany us, while we follow that highway star. It should be really groovy."

"Yeah," the father said, "We want to live, before we burn out. You could share our motel room, when we stop to sleep," he added, hinting at wanting some threesome action with her. "I got a feeling you have a tush under those jeans, that I'd like to rock and roll all night."

"We'd play in here," Moonbeam added, "But, as you can see, this isn't much of a shaggin' wagon."

"I'm kind of involved," Dawn responded, "I appreciate the offer, but I'm not an easy rider, if you catch my drift."

"Involved?" the man asked, "My wife and I are too...but we're liberated...you know, all about the free love, baby."

"Why so paranoid?" his wife asked, "Don't you think we're hip? Am I not pretty? Give us a chance, before you stone us. Is it because you've never been with a girl? It's all good, sweetie, I'll show you the way. You won't be disappointed. I promise," she said, turning her head to smile at Dawn, while her unruly children persisted in tormenting their guest passenger. "You need to loosen up, baby," she said, "Starfire, do we have any weed, or acid left? That might help expand her mind to the idea."

"You know," he started, "usually, when we find a hot little teeny bopper like you, it's because we get vibes from your body that turn us on," the dirty old man said, as if trying to guilt Dawn into obligated submission. "That was the whole purpose of picking you up, sweet thing."

"That's okay," Dawn said, "I'm flattered, but...no. I think my Summer of Love is over," she said both sarcastically and seriously.

This same mystical force that seemed to choose this vehicle for Dawn to take a ride in, appeared to join in on the popular fad of tormenting her. The car radio had lost the interest of the driver, so he popped in an 8-Track tape, that he took out of the glove compartment, and began to play yet another song from *Heart*. As Dawn now listened to the lyrics of *Dog & Butterfly*, it once again brought her depressed eyes to burn with painful tears, as the words only reminded her further of her all-too-brief relationship with her lost love.

The distraught man and wife looked at each other, as if they were highly offended somehow, that the young Dawn wasn't interested in sleeping with them.

"Why you got to be such a bummer?" Moonbeam asked, becoming more and more volatile, and even a bit hostile, in her tone. "You want to make this a bad trip?" again trying to guilt her into doing what they wanted. "You know, we're on a dime bag budget here. You should show us some gratitude, and quit being such a drag."

"I'm actually dropping a cherry bomb at the moment," Dawn explained, both being honest and trying to turn them off to desiring her, "so I doubt you'd really want to get me into bed right now, anyway."

"Shit," Starfire said, "Is that all? Hell, I don't mind. I mean, Moonbeam might, since it might make it a bit difficult for her to go down on your hoochie koo, but it don't bother me none."

Dawn started to understand why their kids were so miserable to be around. She couldn't believe the things they were saying, right in front of their children. It was bad enough that this creepy couple, who were clearly closer to Reuben's age, was trying to pressure her into hedonistic sex, but it somehow made it much more disgusting for her to see that they were capable of raping her right in front of their two young offspring.

"You could always give him a head trip, if you get my meaning," Moonbeam said.

"That would be nice," Starfire immediately agreed. "Could you dig that, then? Perhaps, afterwards, we can all get in a stranglehold together," he added, continuing to make excessive references to Casey Kasem's *Top 40* hits.

Dawn only understood about half of what this pushy couple was saying, but the parts she did understand, was more than enough to make her uncomfortable being in the car with them. When Dawn didn't answer right away, Moonbeam got even more agitated with her.

"Well, what's it going to be, little girl?" Moonbeam asked her. "Do you feel like we do?"

"No offense," Dawn said, secretly eager to teach these people a lesson, and starting to feel better than okay with planning on taking their ride, clothes and mullah, "but I don't know you people. Why can't we be friends?"

"That's okay, Moonbeam," he said, "If she doesn't want to visit the head shop, we can't make her," he said sarcastically, referring to his over exaggerated, over hyped, dick.

"That aint' cool, baby. That aint' jim dandy. You were generous enough to give this chick a free ride. The least she could do is give you some afternoon delight, and not be such an ungrateful barracuda. We don't know her either, but what better way to get to know someone than taking them to bed? She's making me feel like she's taken us for a couple of chumps. You know what...we need to stop picking up these young hitchhikers, baby. You're too nice to these girls, baby. No more Mr. Nice Guy, " she said, conveying intense emotion that wasn't so sweet.

"So..." the husband asked, trying a little too late to lighten the mood, "Where are you from?" he inquired, as he drove the car down the highway. "We should at least be able to carry on friendly conversation, while I drive us all into that waterloo sunset, right?" he said, clearing his throat, as if suddenly embarrassed of how he had been talking to his alluring hitchhiker. "We're going to need to stop in a little while, so the kids can do some candy hunting, but that won't take long, and then we'll be back on the road."

"That reminds me," Moonbeam started, "Shouldn't you be in school right now, sweetheart? What'd you do, runaway?"

Suddenly, the two shameless, negligent parents no longer heard a peep from their otherwise rambunctious kids. Turning around to see if they had abruptly fallen asleep, they saw both of their children decapitated, with blood splattered all over the back seat, and all over Dawn's face, hands, and clothes. Dawn looked at them with a barbarous glare, as her salivating mouth hung wide open, in a fiendish grin, exposing her crimson-stained teeth. Her mystical blue eyes were now as black as pitch.

"I'm an escaped mental patient," she answered.

EPILOGUE
NOVEMBER 1, 1977

It's bright and early, Tuesday morning, on the first of November. A sharp dressed man showed up at the horrendous scene. He was dressed in semi-formal attire that was topped off with a suede trim, plaid blazer, but made a point to not advertise his occupational title. The psychiatric entrance to the hospital is roped off with yellow barricade tape. Several local officers and federal agents are there, scrounging and searching for hints of evidence. The bloodbath had left the facility in ruins, with sections that had been damaged by arson but were luckily contained. Holding his black tie, he ducks under the *Caution* tape, having no clue what awaits his discovery. The FBI had been called in, and were scattered throughout the crime scene, wearing rubber gloves and doing their nauseating duty. As he moves through the chaotic aftermath, he comes upon William's defiled and mangled corpse. William is being thoroughly and intensely examined by one of the seasoned investigators. Suddenly, the other carnage and wreckage seemed insignificant at best.

"Jesus Christ," one of the sickened deputies said, finding the remnants especially revolting. "You would think this had been a goddamn bear attack."

"It was probably a fucking Muslim that did this," he said quietly to himself, while fighting back the urge to cry over his decapitated nephew.

"Excuse me!" Sheriff Morte called out. "Excuse me!" he yelled again, following after the trespasser, who simply and blatantly ignored him.

Sheriff Morte finally caught up and tapped the unwelcome intruder on the back. "Hey, this is a crime scene investigation, asshole. I don't care what bullshit tabloid you're with. Get the Hell out!"

"My name is Agent Shelling. I'm the lead investigator on this case," he said, turning around and flashing the presumptuous Sheriff his pocket badge.

"Oh," the Sheriff said, stepping back to give him his space. "I'm sorry, sir. I didn't know who you were," he promptly apologized, oblivious to the fact that this FBI agent had a conflict of interest with one of the murdered victims.

"Do you have any promising leads?" he asked the embarrassed Sheriff, who was too focused on his mistake to hear his question. "Hey?!" the Fed probed again, "Major Tom? Anyone home?" he asked disparagingly while snapping his fingers in the humiliated Sheriff's face. "Do-you-have-any-breaks-in-the-case?" he asked much slower this time around.

"We haven't been able to find a single print of anyone who wasn't supposed to be here. There are no witnesses, at least none which are willing to talk."

"So, I take it your answer is No then?" Agent Shelling asked, daunting and discouraged.

"We have no solid evidence to direct us to the responsible party. There is also no ballistic element, since there was no gunplay. We did, however, uncover some interesting…um…not quite sure how to put…"

"What? What is it?" Agent Shelling asked frantically and impatiently.

"Well…there's only one mental patient who remains unaccounted for. We can't substantiate that she is the killer, but it has raised a red flag. For all we know, she was a casualty like the rest of them, and just happened to be the only one that the killer saw fit to dispose of. We frankly don't know either way…but,"

"Give me what you have on her," Agent Shelling insistently interrupted. "Do you have a case file on this ~~bitch~~patient?" he urgently inquired, already labeling her as Public Enemy #1 in his own mind. He had taken it upon himself to be both her judge and jury, and had already slammed down the gavel. His only concern was revenge, even if the justice was misdirected or unconfirmed. Someone had to pay for the barbaric execution of his troubled nephew, and he didn't necessarily care whom that turned out to be.

"You know I…" the inadequate Sheriff began again, no match for this vindictive Uncle. The Sheriff could see that this Fed meant business, and was not going to tolerate anything but forthright cooperation. In fact, Sheriff Morte hastily grew suspicious of Agent Shelling, as he could indisputably detect a searing animosity in his eyes, which could only be paralleled to homicidal tendencies.

"And don't give me that jurisdiction nonsense," Agent Shelling forewarned, not letting on that he had a personal stake in this case.

"Her name is Dawn Moon," the Sheriff coughed up in a faint murmur, making an earnest effort to be discreet. "She has no criminal record to speak of. She's a preacher's kid, whose father lives and practices in Silver Spring. There's something else, which has our department completely baffled," the Sheriff said, still reluctant to divulge what he needed to share with the Bureau.

"What? Goddammit! What?!" Agent Shelling interrogated.

"Well…we have found several traces of animal hair, spread throughout the interior of the ward."

"Animal hair?" the Agent asked, uncertain that he heard the Sheriff right.

"Yeeaahh. That's not all, I'm afraid. Our lab has already analyzed it," the Sheriff confessed in just above a whisper.

"Yeah? And?"

"It's wolf hair," the Sheriff said, knowing how crazy that sounded.

***

Dawn furiously digs a grave in the woods, using nothing but her hands. As she throws the dismembered corpses of the flower people into the six-foot pit, she screams at the top of her lungs, venting her unfulfilled fury at her road kill.

"You dig?! You dig?! Huh? Do you dig, mother fucker?! Dig your way out of that, you sorry pieces of shit!" she yells as she pushes and kicks the mound of dirt back into the grave, burying the unsuspecting yet nettling family. She had diced and chopped them up, using nothing but her teeth and her claws.

When she was done, she slumped down beside the freshly filled grave. She had completely exhausted herself. She looks down to see her razor sharp claws covered in soil and dried blood. The dirty girl brings her hands up in front of her face, and licks them, both back and front. The day's events flashed before her tired eyes in explicit, graphic detail. Though Dawn had said her goodbyes to her stolen soulmate, she knew in her broken heart that she would never get over losing him. He would eternally be a part of her, and he would never truly be dead as long as she kept him alive in her.

As Dawn walks back to the rusted, green Station Wagon, soaked to the bone in her confirmed dark and disturbed reality, it begins to shower down rain. Not only does the night sky help cloak the blood that she was coated with from head to toe, but now Heaven itself was either crying for or pissing on her, but either way, it was doing its job. As the born-again serial killer was washed clean by the pouring down rain, the young American Indian stood feet away from the waiting vehicle, and just let the inclement weather do what she needed it to.

"Hahahaha," she laughed mildly hysterically, "Woohoo! When it rains, it pours!" she said, grateful for the rainfall, while caught back by the ironic parallel. Taking a moment or two to just appreciate nature's salvation, she stretched her arms out at her sides, and just like Lynda Carter in *Wonder Woman*, spun around like a top, but without magically changing outfits and with her head tilted back, giggling and squinting at the dark sky above her.

As the rain fell like needles and refused to let up, she undressed right in the middle of the road. Popping the trunk, she found an unlocked suitcase, which included women's clothes inside. She threw the soiled ones in the back seat, and after rinsing all the blood off her birthday suit, dressed in the new threads, right there in the delivering rain. As Dawn bared her ravishing self to the world, nobody seemed to notice, or if they did, they played as if they didn't. Cars and trucks passed by, and either they didn't see her, or they didn't care. This surprised her, but she was certainly in no position to complain. Dawn drove, not having any focal point of direction or destination, but just eager to put as much distance between her and the crime scene as humanly possible.

***

"We don't want to cause a city wide panic, so please keep this confidential," Sheriff Morte naively pleaded with the happy-go-lucky freelance journalist.

The next morning, the Falls Church Sheriff's Office was literally mobbed with diverse members of the press.

"Son of a bitch!" one of the more perceptive deputies said. "We don't have a choice now, Sheriff. You're going to have to give them something."

"Goddamit," Sheriff Morte sighed, shaking his head and grinding his teeth. "I hate this fucking country. Everyone wants to pull over and watch a fucking train wreck. God bless America," he muttered in shame and contempt.

Though they weren't thrilled about the idea of saying anything at this early stage, the desensitized deputy was correct in that the press conference was going to happen whether the department liked it or not.

"Dawn Moon is currently our only suspect. She is an eighteen-year-old Cherokee half-breed, who was a registered resident of this ward. She has mysteriously vanished without a trace, which at this point is the only reason why she is wanted for questioning. We haven't charged her with any crime, because there is no tangible evidence that she is responsible for this slaughter, but it does put up a red flag that she is the sole inmate unaccounted for," the distressed Sheriff officially stated to the media cameras and audio cassette recorders.

Agent Shelling stood back on the sidelines, psyching himself up for what he aimed to do. His left hand played pocket pool with his semi-aroused manhood, as he wanted Dawn so badly, that he could taste her. He craved bloodshed, and he was going to get it, come Hell or high water. Even if it ultimately meant the death of him, he would avenge his troubled nephew's senseless murder.

"Do you think that this young woman is guilty?" one of the anonymous reporters blurted out to the Sheriff, thereby publicly calling him out and putting him on the spot.

"As a spokesman for law enforcement, I have no cause to point fingers," the Sheriff said. "However, speaking as a husband and a father, where there is smoke...there is usually fire."

As the miscellaneous members of the press continued to bombard the city's police department with questions that were impossible to answer, accusations that were too absurd to be founded, or allegations that were simply not grounded in reality, the distraught Uncle walked to his car and took off down the road, making his way to the state line.

***

Seeing that her dashboard fuel gauge was pointing below the *E* level, she urgently pulled off onto the next Exit, off the Capital Beltway, just before crossing into Maryland and merging onto Interstate 270 North. Dawn pulled up into a *Sunoco* station, behind a white 1973 Pontiac *Trans Am* with a black and blue Firebird decal on the hood. As she used the newly converted self-service pump, she noticed that this particular gas station was conveniently equipped with a small store.

Her eyelids had grown heavy, and she needed to stretch her legs. The rain had settled to a gentle mist, but the wind had replaced it and was considerably relentless. The wind had also made it increasingly difficult for Dawn to recover from the ruthless storm. While others around were pulling their knitted Beanie hats further down their heads, wore puffy gloves on their hands and enveloped themselves in their fur and wool coats, Dawn walked peacefully and comfortably toward the door.

The Lynyrd Skynyrd song, *Tuesday's Gone*, is playing overhead, as the wet but clean Dawn tugs on the shop door and steps inside. It's cool in there, but Dawn feels relaxed and refreshed. The cream-colored cotton, poet-sleeved blouse that Dawn had inherited from Moonbeam's luggage, was saturated with the rain, and therefore showed a clear view of her perky breasts and erect nipples. The doused top also revealed her unnatural body hair, which seemed to somehow go unnoticed. Dawn had no panties on either, but the hip-hugging bellbottoms did a better job at hiding what would otherwise be her camel toe.

Fenton, who had been dragging his elbows on the counter, stood to attention and wasted no time in fantasizing about hitting on Dawn. She perceived that the college-age clerk was lusting after her, as she casually made her way to his counter. While she is out of breath, he is all but speechless, but for entirely different reasons. Fenton had been going to night school, but was suddenly grateful to have this mediocre gig during the day.

"Do you have a restroom here that I could use?" she politely asked, while profusely dripping all over the floor of the establishment.

"Uhh…we d-don't really have a restroom for c-customers right now," he replied, while slightly stuttering, "But you are welcome to use the one in the b-back. It's reserved for employees, but you can use it, if you want? It's…" he paused briefly, "probably cleaner."

"Sure," she said with a friendly smile. "Thanks."

As he guided Dawn back behind the counter, he pointed her in the right direction and left her to do her business in the back room. He enjoyed watching her walk away, while taking mental photographs of her envied backside, so he had reference material for later. Dawn was ridiculously sensational, and the type of girl who would only be achievable in a fantasy or centerfold.

"It's just down there, to the right," he told her. "Take your time. I'm sorry, I'd offer you a towel, but I don't have one here in the shop," he told her.

"It's fine!" she yelled back to him, already shutting the bathroom door behind her. Truth was, he was glad to not accommodate her in drying off, as he instantly grew fond of her drenched and braless look.

Though turned on by the heavenly vision of her, she left behind an odor, which smelled like a wet dog. The gullible clerk sniffed the air, and then squeezed his nostrils with his fingers. He momentarily considered that it might be her, but realized that just didn't add up.

"Not possible," he said pretentiously for his ears only. "No way a fox that fine could smell anything but divine," he said with a grin on his face, while slowly nodding his head, as if deluding himself to think that he had a chance in Hell with a chick of that caliber.

While Dawn had distracted his attention away from his dead-end job, three travelers from down South had strutted into the store, and were now browsing the rack with the comic books, road maps and various pornographic magazines. Duane had picked up the latest issue of *Penthouse*, and was avidly flipping through it. He had already slid a copy of *Hustler* down the front of his pants, concealing it under his heavy, red and black-checkered *Woolrich* hunting shirt. His friend was over in the candy isle, checking out the Topps' *Star Wars* trading cards. Fenton saw the assault rifles strapped proudly to the men's backs, which quickly replaced his lust with fear.

"Look, Duane, they got 'em some *Star Wars* cards. It says there's a stick of gum in the package too! Ain't that some shit?" Wayne told his buck-toothed partner, too easily amused and with a thick, good ol' boy drawl.

"Wayne, you about as useless as tits on a bull," Bodean insulted his blind follower, ashamed to even be associated with him.

"That *Star Wars* shit is unrealistic," Duane added. "How you reckon you tell me that aliens exist up there, when there's barely any intelligent life down here?" said one of the poster boy's for ignorance. "It just don't make no sense."

The music selection changed to disco, and Shaun Cassidy's new hit single, *Da Doo Run Run*, began to play on the wall speaker.

Another customer in the store, who looked to be in his mid-twenties, began to jive and swing to the song, right there in the open. He was dressed in a hot pink tracksuit. His hair was feathered, shoulder-length, and neatly parted in the middle. He was clearly effeminate. This didn't go unnoticed by the three country bigots.

"Hey, boys," Bodean said, "Check it out. Nancy boy over there is having a good ol' time dancing with himself." Bodean was a gruff man, burly in size, and was obviously the domineering one in the bunch. He was bald on the top of his head, and wore a backwards *NRA* ball cap and a heavy camouflage coat.

"This is the same dude that sings that song, *Hey Deanie*...you know...*Deanie*...like your name? It's off his new album, *Born Late*."

"I swear, boy, if you don't shut the fuck up real quick, I'm gonna see to it that you're dead early." Bodean threatened. "How the fuck do you know who this is, anyway? You listenin' to this faggity music behind my back?"

"No, Bo," Duane lied, nervously. "I just caught a bit of his stuff by accident, while tuning the radio to George Jones and Mickey Gilley."

"Yeah, I better not catch you listening to anything other than down home Country-Western, or so help me

God, I'm gonna hit you so hard, you'll be dancing with that queer-bait over there."

Bo quickly turned his attention back to what he saw as a dancing queen. "You need some help bringing some of them *Ho Hos* up to the check-out, retard? It must be tough, boy, trying to hold anything with that limp wrist."

Bo's friends joined him in laughing at the kid, while Wayne ran over and grabbed a box of the *Hostess* snack cakes, and pelted it at the back of his head. The cowardly cashier slumped down and hunched over, looking at the counter to avoid eye contact with the homophobe bullies.

"He probably can't hear you, Bo," Wayne said. "He got them ears muffled up by that long hair."

The innocent customer had grown weary of the unwarranted attacks, and decided to leave. As he attempted to make his way to the exit, Duane stuck his leg out and tripped him. The gay pacifist was able to catch himself from falling flat on his face, but lost control of his balance and incidentally collided into Bodean, which only made matters worse.

"Oh no you didn't," Bodean said, aggressively grabbing the guy by his zippered top, as his gross intolerance had reached its boil. "I know you didn't just get all those sissy germs on me." The frightened young man looked Bodean in the eyes, which only further infuriated the proud supremacist. Bodean spit on the young man, nailing him right on his mustache. Bo lifted him at least six inches off the floor, and threw him violently into the *ICEE* machine, causing the defenseless homosexual to bang the side of his head on the rigid counter and then the even harder floor.

Bodean stepped up to the checkout counter, to devote a moment to harassing the spectating clerk. "Why don't you get a haircut?" he asked rhetorically, pathetically offended by Fenton's long hair. "Are you a faggot too?"

Dawn was squatting over the toilet, careful not to actually let her luscious ass touch the seat. As she peed, she stuck her hands in her urine stream, rubbing them together to better clean the gore and grime off her hands and from underneath her fingernails.

Wayne had been looking at some leftover Halloween masks that were still for sale, and picked one up that was supposed to be *Pocahontas*. The mask was made of cheap, thin plastic, with holes cut out for the eyes. He pulled the string of elastic back and fit the mask over his face.

"Hey, look at me guys," Wayne said. "I'm a little Indian brave," he said, as he pranced around the store, skipping along while mimicking the stereotypical Indian chant with his hand. "Hiya-ya-ya. Hi-ya-ya-ya."

Just then, the three pranksters simultaneously spotted Dawn, who had been silently watching from behind the counter.

"Oh baby, looks like the Great Spirit outdid himself with this one," Duane complimented her remarkable beauty.

"Well, I'll be a monkey's uncle," Bodean said. "We got ourselves a feathered piece of tail up in here. What do you say, youngun? You want to come over here and smoke on my peace pipe?"

"I hear that! My totem pole is pitching a teepee right now," Wayne boasted.

"Sorry," Dawn said calmly but firmly, "I don't date hicks. You're not my type."

"You have quite the little mouth on you, don't you honey? Would you like something to put in it?" Bodean asked as he grabbed his bulge through his soiled and stained blue jeans, while his friends snickered and chuckled.

Dawn suddenly fell into a trance, as if time had frozen still. She found herself trapped in a daydream where she indulged in a violent fantasy. She imagined herself throwing all caution to the wind and recklessly letting loose on this chauvinist redneck. She envisioned herself making him reap her whirlwind of wrath, as she literally ripped him to shreds. As everyone around her screamed in unfathomable terror, she used Bodean's blood as war paint on her face. She yanked his femur bone out of his open thigh, and held it up above her head. She howled out a victory roar, while shaking the bigot's bone like a tomahawk.

As Dawn relished in this dazed state, she began to feel the tiny hairs on her arms stand at attention, as she felt a presence brush by her that was chilling...but not physically, just spiritually. She began to hear tribal-like drumbeats, which were subtle at first, but got louder. Her flesh had goose bumps, but not from being cold. Once she decided against acting on her impulse of rage, the unidentified presence subsided and disappeared.

As tempting as this vivid pre-meditation was, she knew she couldn't risk the consequences. Her priority needed to be one of self-preservation. She was a fox on the run, and no gun-obsessed hick was going to spoil that.

When she came out of her mirage, she had been scratching her face, furiously but subconsciously. The three hillbillies had been watching her while she had been stuck in her spell. They had even thrown some things at her, which just bounced off her face and chest. They couldn't snap her out of it, while she was still trapped inside her own head.

"Psycho," Bodean said, looking her up and down with disdain and disgust, while the young cashier still ogled her perfectly shaped ass. "Look-see here, boys. We have a daydream believer on our hands."

"I'd like to have her in my hands," Duane said, as Fenton nodded his head in silent agreement, while doing what he could to help the violated customer who had been knocked out cold.

"I'm sure one of your potbellied country queers can help you out," she said boldly, resisting the urge to act on her impulse to make the world a better place by ridding it of such white trash.

"Look, bitch," Bo began, "You stink like a varmint, but you're also hotter than a goat's butt in a pepper patch." He was so close that Dawn could smell his rancid breath, as his breathing got much heavier. "I'm fixin' to rip those britches right off you, and make you one of my kin."

"If you're hoping to intimidate me, you're going to be sadly disappointed," she said, staring back at him without a flinch.

"Grab her titty, Bo!" one of his friends shouted cheerfully, egging him on toward sexual assault.

"You do," Dawn warned, "And you'll leave here with one less hand. So, I strongly suggest if you value your life, to turn around, walk out, and go suck off one of your toothless friends."

Bo looked deep into her eyes, with the intention of giving her one final chance at surrendering her will, before he raped her right there in the store. However, when he saw the volatile darkness in her eyes, his sinister agenda swiftly backfired.

"What are you?" Bo asked her, now taking a step back and changing his tone, suddenly missing his promiscuous wife and three kids who secretly weren't even his.

"Leave," Dawn said again, "or the three of you will find out."

Dawn watched through the glass door, as the redneck trio got in their 1975 Ford *Ranger* F250 pickup and boastfully revved their engine a few times, before high tailing out of there. Dawn looked down and observed the Mississippi vanity plate on the rear of the truck, which read *BUMKIN*.

Dawn resumed to browsing, as if nothing had happened. She came across a box of glazed donuts, which reminded her of how Reuben had felt inside her, as if she ever needed reminding.

Meanwhile, Fenton hears a government-issued transmission that interferes with the station that had been providing the in-store music:

"We bring you this emergency bulletin to warn the citizens of the East Coast that Dawn Moon, an 18-year-old Native American, is wanted for questioning in connection with the massacre that happened at a psychiatric ward in Falls Church, Virginia. We at *WDCE-FM* have been tasked with broadcasting this over the air, in hopes that somebody somewhere will see this potentially dangerous suspect, and immediately contact the FBI. I'm told that if this Dawn Moon does not voluntarily turn herself in to the authorities within the next 24 hours, the FBI will conduct a nationwide manhunt, using all their resources and manpower to expedite the effort. Highway perimeters are already being put into action. Please be careful and proceed with extreme caution."

The young cashier, who had left his counter to rush to the injured customer's aid, pulls up on his turtleneck collar, as if that would somehow help shield him from the alleged maniac in his store. He knew it was her that they were talking about, and swallowed heavily as she approached the counter.

"You want to ring me up?" she asked him, acting as if she hadn't just heard that radio broadcast, and pretended to not be worried about leaving loose ends.

"Don't worry about it," Fenton told her. "It's on me."

"Are you sure?" she asked for verification.

"Yeah," he paused briefly. "It's cool."

"Thank you," Dawn said smiling, "I appreciate that."

"No," he corrected her, "Thank you." Fenton moved his eyes down to her feet and noticed her clogs. They had been the only article of clothing that she had overlooked, and therefore she had seen no need to change. The light colored clogs were stained with blood.

As she began to walk away, he called out to her. "Hey, Dawn...I think you're a groovy chick," the quivering employee said nervously, trying to fake some level of confidence and courage. "I don't know what you've done or why," Fenton said, as she was halfway out the door, but could still hear him. "But, whatever you do, don't go back there. Run, run as far as your feet will carry you."

Dawn just glanced back at him warmly, and smiled in gratitude, before walking out the door to do just that.

Fenton held the young man in his arms, who was still unresponsive. The stranger's head was bleeding profusely, and Fenton prayed that the guy would miraculously survive until the cops arrived. As he rocked the victim back and forth, he thought of his family and how he regretted not having appreciated them more. His father was a rodeo cowboy, and had competed in the *Hesston National Finals* in 1975.

After an unfortunate falling out with his father, about the debatable war in Vietnam, Fenton had run away, leaving his life in Oklahoma behind him. He had gone to great lengths to evade the Draft, and his father didn't find that to be honorable, which sparked the argument that would estrange their relationship. But after witnessing the deplorable display of so-called 'Southern charm' in his store, he realized that his father wasn't so bad. Though he didn't see eye to eye with his conservative father on many issues, particularly about the American condition, Fenton took comfort in knowing that his parents would never treat fellow human beings this way, which made him proud of his very different Southern heritage.

"We're not all like that," Fenton said, as his eyes flooded with salty tears, looking down at the dead face he still cradled in his arms. "We're not all like that," he repeated, though the flamboyant fatality couldn't hear his heartfelt words of reassurance.

As Dawn moved on down Interstate 270, she was struck with a case of the munchies. Reaching back behind her, she grabbed one of the bags of snacks that she had gotten from the convenient store. She opened the Nabisco box of *Zu Zu Ginger Snaps*, and took a handful to nibble on while she drove. She found the wafers to be tasteless. She then opened the glass bottle of her *Sun-Rise* orange soda, but once again couldn't taste any flavor.

"Well, fuck it. They wouldn't call it junk food if it wasn't meant to be thrown away," she said aloud to herself, as she rolled down the window and threw the soda pop out of the moving vehicle.

Dawn continued to drive the Chevy *Townsman* Wagon as fast as she could without risking police intervention, going just above 55mph. She knew that she would inevitably encounter obstruction interference, but she would cross that bridge much sooner than expected. Hearing a siren, as if it had come out of nowhere, she looked in the rearview mirror and saw a police cruiser tailgating her. Not wishing to draw more attention to herself, she obediently complied and pulled off to the left shoulder. When she stopped the car, she hit the brakes hard and sudden.

"Do you know why I pulled you over, miss?" the officer asked, stepping up to her driver's window.

Dawn had finally just begun to dry off, with the heater running at maximum temperature. Dawn's head was face down into the steering wheel, as if she was comatose. The concerned officer leaned forward, to get a better look at her.

"Miss? Can you hear me? I pulled you over to give you a citation for littering. Are you drunk?"

Dawn's window was rolled up, so the officer decided to open her door, to take a closer look at the situation. As he did this, Dawn rose up, grabbed him by the wrist, and yanked him in the car. While holding him still with her superhuman adrenaline, she bit his neck and severed a major artery. As he bled like a fountain, she sucked and swallowed what came out, this time being extra careful not to get any on her outfit. When she had enough, she pushed him away, letting him fall onto the street beside her.

"AAHH," she sighed, as she leaned her head back against the headrest. "That's much better. That bacon hit the spot," she said, as she savored the pork flavor.

ABOUT THE AUTHOR

Nicholas Knight was born 'Sean Delorie,' in 1972 and was raised in Sterling, Virginia. Even at an early age, he knew that he was different. He was always drawn to the creative arts, and never had much of an aptitude for the academics. Nicholas was blessed with a wild imagination, and cursed with a heart of gold. Following his unbearably painful second divorce, to a brilliant sociopath named Heather - whom he tragically loved deeply (who proved to be a proud adulterer, pathological liar, a sadistic identity thief, and a ruse in every way imaginable), he began putting his inner torment and agony into writing and acting. They say that the best writers write about what they know, which is precisely what Nicholas has done and continues to do. That said, his books tend to carry elements of religion, politics, horror, superhero and supernatural fantasy, and erotic romance. He has also attempted to write and illustrate children's books.

Nicholas is much more than a novelist. He is an avid political activist and broken, yet faithful Christian, which make for an unusual and outspoken combination. He's had to learn that the American Christian community, for the most part, is superficial, sanctimonious and discriminatory; and the majority of women he has known are cold and brutal. He lives alone, with traumatizing regret and detrimental despair. We all make mistakes, but unlike Heather's crimes against him, his are not boastful. His past choices can never be redeemed or forgiven; and knowing this is what keeps him up at night. His entire life, he has been aching to love, but has unfortunately often attracted and invested his feelings in women who love to harm. These countless betrayals sadly led him to eventually hurt the people he would love the most and the very few who would love him back.

The decisions we make in life will always define us, if not immediately, then eventually. These choices will usually either humble or harden us. He has to fight every day to resist allowing the latter to assume control. Nicholas has been backstabbed by those he has trusted more times than he can list, but what kills him the most are the few he's hurt himself. Most people fall in love once. Most people die once. Nicholas has died three times, as this love would always prove to leave him or be taken from him. He learned that his future would be filled with loss and disappointment. He was bullied as early as 3rd grade, being called *Frankenstein* for his oversized head. He didn't gain the attention of a girl until he was 18. Little did he know then, that he would pay a heavy price for this female affection that he craved so desperately. While his chain of tragedy and adversity would later make for vivid stories and intense performances, it would also inevitably crush his afflicted spirit.

Nicholas is drawn to the darkness, as an artist, primarily due to his soul being repeatedly crushed by rejection and his world being damaged by endless affliction. His life has not been an easy road, but his debilitating fear of his own mortality, his deep love for his daughter, and his desire to not be forgotten, keep him pushing forward, despite the obstacles and heartaches that consistently fall into his lap. Tormented with fraudulent passion and callous betrayal, he would use his endless suffering to mold himself into a stronger entertainer. Nicholas hopes that his ship will finally come in, and that these acting opportunities will inevitably result in launching a career. His dream is to make something of his writing, either for print or for the screen. He believes in himself, and feels confident in his storytelling ability.

Nicholas is a doting father who wishes he could have held on to Andrea (Harley's stunning mother, who unfortunately turned out not to want him). Nicholas is an exceptional actor and a brilliant writer, and continues to pursue these two endeavors for his daughter more than for himself. It's been a real struggle, but he is determined to keep trying, until someone out there is willing to give him a real chance at making something of himself. Despite Heather's continuous sabotage and irreparable malice, he tries to use whatever money he makes to pay the bills and make his visitations with Harley as memorable as possible. He is the definition of the term *starving artist*, and has become even more so since meeting the malignant Heather, who still continues to attack him with fraud. His dream is to be financially independent, where he can take care of himself and his daughter. He genuinely appreciates your support and hopes you enjoy his work both on the printed page and on the big screen. www.imdb.me/nicholasknight.

OTHER GREAT TITLES FROM

Burning Bulb
PUBLISHING

WWW.BURNINGBULBPUBLISHING.COM

BELLY TIMBER

From the writers of Darkened Hills, Detour to Armageddon and Night of the Living Dead comes a novel unlike any other...

In the 1800's, ordinary people learned the secret of the Kala and undertook extraordinary measures to rid the earth of this evil. This is their story.

For John McCormick, life on the Indiana frontier held nothing but promise. His settlement along the White River would soon become the crossroads of America. Friends and family from back in Ohio and other points east were all making plans to see what all the fuss was about in the newly-formed city of Indianapolis. Yes, things were good. John had his general store and his friend George Pogue had his blacksmith business. Claims were being staked and relations with the native Indians were amicable. The town was growing and nothing could be better... or so he thought.

In Ohio, an evil was brewing. The Lecky Family, a group of ruthless Mongolian nomads, had made their way to America and were practicing their cannibalistic religion of Kala with reckless abandon. No one was safe, not even John McCormick's family.

Burning Bulb
PUBLISHING

Bob Gray's
ATTACK OF THE
MELONHEADS
NOVELIZATION BY
SOLON TSANGARAS & GARY LEE VINCENT

BOB GRAY'S ATTACK OF THE MELONHEADS

Fifty years ago, a doctor sought to cure a terrible disease. Hidden from the world, Doctor Malcolm Crowe toiled in the dead of night while the world was sleeping, creating a new breed of mutant—all in the name of science.

Yes, he thought he could cure the sick children. But he was wrong.

Today, the results of his cruel and unconventional experiments have manifested into an evil never before seen.

Now, in Kirtland, Ohio, the town's unsuspecting residents are about to encounter the full onslaught of this unimaginable terror.

Can something be done before it's too late?

Burning Bulb
PUBLISHING

GARY LEE VINCENT'S
DARKENED
THE WEST VIRGINIA VAMPIRE SERIES

DARKENED HILLS

When evil descends on a small West Virginia town, who will survive?

Jonathan did not start out his life to become a rambler, it just worked out that way. William was a troubled youth with something to hide. Both were from Melas, a small town tucked away in the West Virginia hills... a town where disappearances are happening more and more frequently.

After the suicide of a wanted serial killer, the townsfolk thought the nightmare was over. But when a centuries-old vampire is discovered they find out the hard way it's just getting started. Dark secrets can only stay hidden for so long and when the devil comes to collect, there will be hell to pay. Can Jonathan and William find a way to stop the vampire before it's too late? Find out in *Darkened Hills!*

DARKENED HOLLOWS

In the heart-stopping sequel to the award-winning *Darkened Hills*, Jonathan and William must return to West Virginia to face possible criminal charges stemming from their last visit to the damned town of Melas, where both had narrowly escaped the clutches of a vampire seethe.

And as livestock start mysteriously getting murdered with all of their blood drained, worried farmers are searching for answers - leaving the local Sheriff and his deputy racing against time to learn the cause before a more violent crime is committed.

Burning Bulb
PUBLISHING

WWW.DARKENEDHILLS.COM

WOL-VRIEY
BIZARRO AND TRANSGRESSIVE FICTION

BOSTON POSH (BUD MALONE #1)

In 2028 AD, the USA is a nation ravaged by hungry dragons and dinosaurs. In Boston, Massachusetts, private eye Bud Malone is hired to rescue a kidnapped heiress. But nothing is as it seems.

Malone works to unravel a tangled web involving Boston Chinatown, a 200-year-old woman with a 9-year-old body, white robots, a human-liver-eating psychopath, a golem, a porcelain dragon, and a snake goddess with a crush on him. There's also a woman obsessed with chicken sex. Then Malone meets Posh Lane, a gorgeous call girl who's desperate to quit her pimp.

Romantic sparks ignite between Posh and Malone, but Posh's past suddenly catches up with her in a BIG way. To save Posh, Malone agrees to run a quest for Earth's new rulers, the Forks. But, Malone has no idea that agreeing to the Fork's odd request will send him on the weirdest trip he's ever been on in his life.

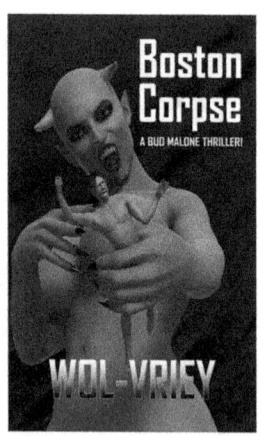

BOSTON CORPSE (BUD MALONE #2)

MAGIC CAN BE MURDER! - Drag queen Lucy Tang is back in Boston, and is hell-bent on settling her vindetta against casino owner Sookie Ling. And suddenly, Bud Malone, PI, has the case of his life to resolve.

When Boston's robot police force are baffled by a mind transfer case, they come to Malone for help. The one person who can likely help Malone out here is the witch Soledad Bathory. But Soledad seems to know a lot more than she's telling him. It's a case not made easier when Malone meets Soledad's beautiful cousin, Josephine 'Slave' Bailey. Slave has her own plans for Malone, most of which involve teaching him BDSM and making him her new Master.

Oh, and Rick Rogers owes Sookie Ling a whole lot of money, a gambling debt that's going to be literally Hell to pay!

BOSTON CORPSE - Not your average detective novel!

Burning Bulb
PUBLISHING

WOL-VRIEY
BIZARRO AND TRANSGRESSIVE FICTION

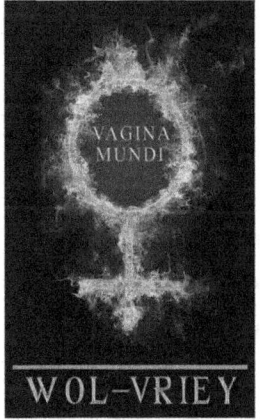

VAGINA MUNDI

Rachel Risk is a professional thief with super-strong hair that can stretch like tentacles to manipulate objects. Ashley Status has both a digitally augmented brain, and 'muscle-purses' in her arms and legs in which she stores inflatable objects—cars, guns, rocket launchers, etc.

When Raye is framed as the fall girl in a jewel robbery, the pair flee Chicago's vengeful robot gangsters and take refuge in the Hotel Bizarre, where the gorgeous 'vagina singer,' Femina, is performing for a week.

But the Hotel Bizarre is even stranger than its name suggests, and very soon Raye and Ash are involved in an deadly adventure, a struggle for survival the likes of which they'd never imagined possible—with loads of deviant sex, drugs, music, and violence at every turn. And just what is the old woman in the skin desert really doing with all those cats glued to her walls?

VAGINA MUNDI—a Bizarro Hymn in praise of WOMAN!

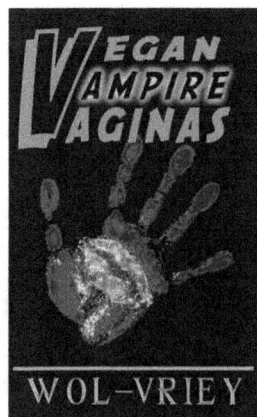

VEGAN VAMPIRE VAGINAS

The biggest bank heist in US history. And Tom Palmer can't remember pulling it off. And no, this isn't your standard case of amnesia. After a one-night-stand gone horribly wrong, Boston salesman Tom Palmer wakes up with a vagina implanted in his left hand. Then his day gets worse.

Tom is transported across space-time to a nightmare version of Boston, one where the Bizarro virus has transformed half the population into cannibals. Worst of all, Tom discovers that in this new Boston, he's the infamous gangster Pussypalm, wanted for robbing the Federal Reserve Bank of Boston a year ago. He also learns that the vagina in his hand is prophetic, i.e. it talks . . . after sex.

With 130 people left dead during his bank heist and six billion dollars missing, Tom knows he's living on borrowed time. It is in his best interests not to remember anything. Because once he does . . .

Burning Bulb
PUBLISHING

WOL-VRIEY
BIZARRO AND TRANSGRESSIVE FICTION

VEGAN ZOMBIE APOCALYPSE

In the post-apocalypse worlderness, zombies rule the earth. They're allergic to meat, and brains literally make them explode. Zombies now eat blood potatoes, parasitic tubers grown in the flesh of humancows corralled in maximum security farms. Two fugitives meet in the ancient ruins of Texas. The first is Soil 15-f, a womancow who's escaped her farm a week before she's due to be killed and her blood potato crop harvested. The second fugitive is Able Kane, former head necros food technician, now sentenced to death for heresy. But Soil is no ordinary humancow.

Unknown to herself, she's the vegan zombie agricultural revolution, and the zombies desperately want her back. And the necros equally desperately want Able Kane dead. He's fled with a forbidden discovery which will reshape the world for the worse if used. And Able is just hardheaded/misguided enough to use it.

MELANIE NEMESIS CATCHPOLE

In Springfield, Massachusetts, Melanie Catchpole is hired to fetch back a magic teddy bear worth millions of dollars from a warehouse across town. Problem is, the warehouse is down in Springfield's O-Zone-that totally weird sector of the city where Bizarro fell to Earth. The 'O' is a fairytale land, a place where dreams and nightmares literally live and breathe.

Worse still, the gingers—mutant cannibals—prowl the O. The gingers have already eaten everyone else Melanie's employers sent to get back the magic teddy bear.

Accompanied by the handsome but ruthless Doug Fisher (who she finds sexy but doesn't dare entrust her heart to), Melanie enters the O-Zone. Melanie and Doug are instantly caught up in an adventure they'd never have believed credible even if written as fiction . . . and Melanie's used to experiencing the very weird as the norm.

And now, additionally, there's a mystery to unravel: What does the dark, freezing-cold being called The Fixer want with Mary, the barkeep's daughter?

Burning Bulb

WOL-VRIEY
BIZARRO AND TRANSGRESSIVE FICTION

BIG TROUBLE IN LITTLE ASS

From Bizarro master storyteller Wol-vriey comes a truly weird western tale that will leave you awe-struck and on the edge of your seat...

In the town named Little Ass, tight-assed prostitute Rosa overhears a gunslinger's plans to assassinate rancher Edison Bennett. Once the badass Bennett learns of the plot, he ensures there'll be hell to pay for any attempt on his life!

Yes, it's going to take all of gunslinger Jude's shooting prowess, his eclectic collection of strange firearms, a trusty horse that requires an owners' manual, and the help of the lovely and invigorating Nell (who's EXTREMELY odd when the going gets weird), to survive the Bizarro hell that Edison Bennett unleashes in order to hold onto the land that he'd stolen from Madam Zizi.

BIZARRO 101 (A BASIC PRIMER)

Welcome to the strange place:

A collection of 37 flash fiction stories designed to introduce one to the Bizarro/New Weird Genre.

Weird, dreamy, nightmarish, absurd, sad, surreal, humorous . . . this collection of tales is all this and more.

***

"This primer is the very essence of any and all styles and types of Bizarro writing. Wol-vriey collects, distills, and bottles up these 37 tiny stories for your sensory enjoyment. This is an absolute must-read for anyone new to the genre, because it demonstrates the scope of what Bizarro is, and what it can be."
                    –Teresa Pollack, Bizarro commentator and blogger

Burning Bulb
PUBLISHING

ANTHOLOGIES
BIZARRO AND TRANSGRESSIVE FICTION

THE BIG BOOK OF BIZARRO

The Big Book of Bizarro brings together the peculiar prose of an international cast of the most grotesquely-gonzo, genre-grinding modern writers who ever put pen to paper (or mouse to pad), including:

NIGHT OF THE LIVING DEAD horror writers John Russo & George Kosana; HUSTLER MAGAZINE erotica contributors Eva Hore, Andrée Lachapelle, & J. Troy Seate and established Bizarro genre authors D. Harlan Wilson, William Pauley III, Wol-vriey, Laird Long, Richard Godwin and so many more!

From Alien abductions to Zombie sex, The Big Book of Bizarro contains OVER FIFTY STORIES of the most outrélandish transgressive fiction that you'll ever lay your capricious and curious hands upon!

WESTWARD HOES

Nine outlaw writers rode into town from obscurity to pen nine tantalizing tales of horror and fantasy, and leaving once they branded their own personal marks on the weird western genre and became living legends of the American Frontier experience.

Like drunken Indian scouts, the writers fervidly tracked down and captured the Western genre, tore off its fashionable veneer and ravished its exposed essence.

So belly up to the bar with your favorite soiled dove and enjoy perusing these thrilling tales of Old West debauchery, danger and desire; compiled by the publisher of The Big Book of Bizarro and featuring the bizarro novella *Big Trouble in Little Ass* by Wol-vriey.

Burning Bulb
PUBLISHING

DETOUR TO ARMAGEDDON BY SOLON TSANGARAS

"An all-pervasive breakout of ghoulish pandemonium related
with unbridled glee and terror."
—John Russo, author of *Night of the Living Dead*

WHO WILL SURVIVE? WILL THEY WANT TO?

Enter a world where your best friend, your neighbor, your mother
or father, just aren't the same people you knew. But THEY aren't the
real enemy...

Join groups of survivors as they make their way across this
once-great nation that has been devastated by a man-made plague
created by corporate greed and fed by self-serving men who are
hungry for power and control.

Burning Bulb
PUBLISHING

DAVID J. FAIRHEAD

THE FALL

Hopelessness... How do you protect your loved ones when Hell itself opens its insidious mouth?

Horror... Nightmarish Creatures invade your world and there is nowhere to hide.

Blood... How long can you hold out before they come for you?

Pain... Where do you run to avoid being eaten alive by monsters with a voracious appetite for your flesh?

Screams... While you selfishly run for your own life.

Questions... Who is to blame? Where did they come from? How many people survived...and how does the human race find the means to fight back?

THE FALL OF TOMORROW is man's last tale of desperation told by those that are striving to salvage some hope against a ravenous bastion of evil beasts bent on ruling our world.

DWELLING IN THE DARK

From David J. Fairhead, author of the FALL OF TOMORROW, comes DWELLING IN THE DARK- A soulful anthology of creeping terror to keep you up in the small hours with horror set in the past, present and future. Overlapping bits of puzzle fitting each other, before and after The Fall of Tomorrow.

A place where three children facing a monstrous foe can only pray that their bloody summer would just come to an end. Go back to the 1960's- THE COMMUNE where overindulging hippies use a mage's diary to control the end of the world, only to see first-hand that their drug induced visions have horrific ramifications. Where a young boy's visit to a haunted house becomes a lesson in RESIDUAL morality. The story, DEEPER- plunges two brothers into a sinkhole only to find they were being hunted by an insidious creature from its depths. Visit the old west as hero Dekker Collins battles evil gunslingers in DEMONEYE.

And so much more...!

Burning Bulb
PUBLISHING

WWW. FAIRLYDARKPRODUCTIONS.COM

RISE OF THE DEAD - a collection of seventeen tales of unspeakable zombie terror. Featuring a foreword and short story by John A. Russo!

www.TheJohnRusso.com

Burning Bulb
PUBLISHING

WEST VIRGINIA-THEMED
HUMORROROTICA
BY RICH BOTTLES JR.

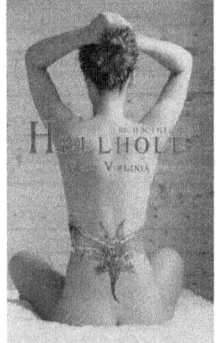

HELLHOLE WEST VIRGINIA

From the heights of Mothman's perch high atop the Silver Bridge in Point Pleasant to the depths of Hellhole Cavern in Pendleton County, evil lurks within the shadows as the sun sets upon the haunted hills and hollows of West Virginia.

Bizarro author Rich Bottles Jr. blows the coffin lid off horror genre clichés with this tour de force cast of Eco-friendly vampires, beach-yearning zombies and sex-starved she-devils.

LUMBERJACKED

If you are easily offended or do not possess a truly depraved sense of humor, this story may not be the light summer reading fare you desire. As for the four feisty female freshmen stranded on top of West Virginia's third highest mountain, they have no choice but to experience the sick, twisted debauchery and perverted mayhem described deep inside the tight unbroken bindings of this horrific missive.

Lumberjacked takes the reader to a nightmarish world where character development and aesthetic integrity are prematurely cut short by the swinging axes of maniacal lumberjacks, who are hell bent on death and destruction in the remote forests of Appalachia. And at the climax, when paranoia crosses over to the paranormal, Lumberjacked makes Deliverance look like a family raft trip down the Lower Gauley.

THE MANACLED

What happens when twin brothers lease out the former West Virginia State Penitentiary with the false purpose of filming a documentary on supernatural phenomena, but their true intention is to make a pornographic movie?

Chaos ensues as the disturbed spirits of murdered convicts, along with the reanimated dead from the neighboring Indian Burial Mound, take their vengeance on the unwary and undressed trespassers.

Zombies, ghosts, mobsters and porn collide in this bizarro tale from horror author Rich Bottles Jr.

Burning Bulb
PUBLISHING

EVERYTHING HERE IS A NIGHTMARE
Collected Works Vol 1.

"Pyles makes it look easy. His characters come instantly alive with the cocksure verve and swagger of rock stars."

> *- Daniel Knauf, creator of HBO's "Carnivale,"*
> *Executive Producer/Writer, ABC's "The Blacklist."*

The critically acclaimed author of Demons, Dolls and Milkshakes returns with fifteen tales of horror and suspense with Everything Here is a Nightmare.

From zombies in the old west, to a young boy tempted by the Devil. From vampires with romantic longing, to an abandoned lighthouse haunted by vengeful spirits. From a serial killer getting unholy justice, to a haunted English race car, Nelson W Pyles invites you to explore a landscape of fear, suspense and horror.

Take his hand and hold on tight. Remember that whatever you find here, whatever you see, no matter what you might think it could be... know this: Everything Here is a Nightmare.

Burning Bulb
PUBLISHING

THE MOST FRIGHTENING MOVIE
EVER MADE IS NOW A NOVEL!

night OF THE
LIVING DEAD

JOHN A. RUSSO

NIGHT OF THE LIVING DEAD

Why does Night of the Living Dead hit with such chilling impact?

Is it because everyday people in a commonplace house are suddenly the victims of a monstrous invasion? Or is it because the ghouls who surround the house with grasping claws were once ordinary people, too?

Decide for yourself as you read, and the horror grips you.

All the cannibalism, suspense and frenzy of the smash-hit move are here in the novel.

www.TheJohnRusso.com

Burning Bulb
PUBLISHING

THE BOOBY HATCH

With NIGHT OF THE LIVING DEAD, John Russo helped blaze a path in the horror genre that has never been equalled. In this hillarious erotic novel, he blazes a path through the wild, zany Sex Revolution of the 1970s.

Sweet, innocent Cherry Jankowski works for Joyful Novelties, where she tests sex toys ranging from the ridiculous to the sublime. But she can't find love or peace of mind and her efforts are hampered by a Peeping Tom, an exhibitionist, a cross-dressing boyfriend, a quack psychiatrist, and even her own product-testing partner, Marcello Fettucini, who can't get it up anymore and is scared of losing his job!

www.TheJohnRusso.com

Burning Bulb
PUBLISHING

Bright little children, at school and at play,
until their minds are stolen away...

A Novel of Terror by

JOHN A. RUSSO

THE ACADEMY

THE ACADEMY

The Academy. It's every parent's dream, turning their little
darlings into geniuses, superachievers, perfect little
children.

And if there's a problem, the Academy fixes that too. It's a
simple operation. Just a little device. Then a teeny pink scar
on a tender little skull . . .

One boy knows the secret. Now he wants his mind back.
But it's much, much too late. Too late for anything but the
ugly feelings. The bad feelings. The messy sexy feelings. The
knife-cold hatred, the murderous rage, for total, screaming,
blood-drenching revenge . . .

www.TheJohnRusso.com

Burning Bulb

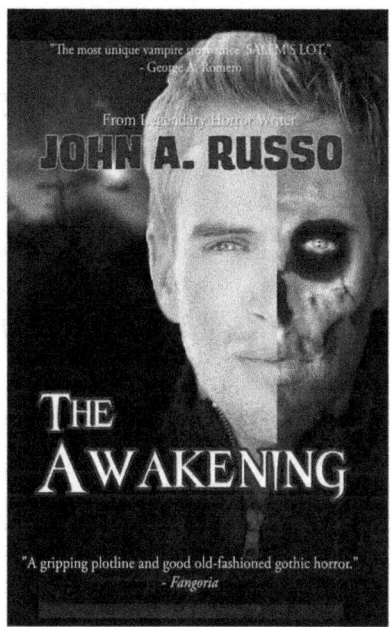

THE AWAKENING

For two hundred years, he has rested. Now he rises. Now he will be satisfied. Nothing can stop him. No one can resist him.

Benjamin Latham is young and handsome, his eighteenth-century mind wakened to a bizarre twentieth-century world. And there is the need deep within . . . an animal need, frightening, murderous, unholy . . . a vital need that must be fed.

And with his need comes a power over men and women to do his bidding, to quiet his dark craving . . .

Until the murders begin. And the inquiries. All suggesting the same hideous truth.

Now Benjamin must find a sanctuary: a lover, a partner, a friend. Someone who can share his darkness. Someone he can lead to . . . The Awakening.

www.TheJohnRusso.com

Burning Bulb

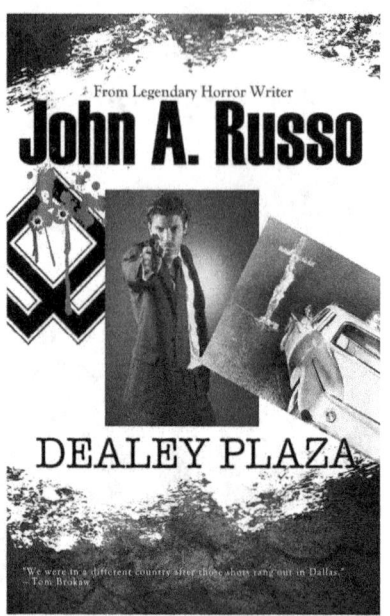

DEALEY PLAZA

From legendary horror and suspense writer JOHN RUSSO comes a harrowing tale where no one is safe!

Dealey Plaza is one of the most notorious places in America, and when youthful conspiracy buffs go there in 1964 to stage their own reenactment of the Kennedy Assassination, four of them are brutally murdered ~ the first victims of a hate-filled legacy that continues for four more decades.

The survivors of that long-ago Dallas trip, each of them now icons of the American way of life, are about to be honored ~ or killed.

Who will live and who will die? Will it be country-western star Lori McCoy? Her loving husband? Her scheming ex-husband? Or the case-hardened FBI agent and longtime friend who risks his life trying to protect them?

www.DealeyPlazaBook.com

Burning Bulb
PUBLISHING

LIVING THINGS

Beneath the shimmering Miami sun sprawls one of the Mafia's biggest empires, a glittering world of lavish beachfront mansions, neon-painted nightclubs, beautiful women, expensive cars—and absolute control over the state's billion-dollar drug trade. But, one by one, its ganglords and henchmen are falling prey to a new rival. His powers are fueled by monstrous ancient rituals; his hellish undead legions slaughter mobsters and innocent citizens alike, his unholy lust for power is virtually unstoppable.

Now a burned-out ex-detective and a brilliant anthropologist must enter a gruesome, nightmare world to fight this master of malevolence and illusion. Their time is short, their weapons few, and they face an ultimate, terrifying choice - annihilation or the loss of their souls to the eternal torment of those who never die. . .

www.TheJohnRusso.com

Burning Bulb
PUBLISHING

ELVIS PRESLEY, CIA ASSASSIN BY ANDY RAUSCH

"I can guarantee you. Read this book and you'll never look at Elvis the same way again!"
~ Douglas Brode, author of ELVIS CINEMA AND POPULAR CULTURE

SOON TO BE A MAJOR MOTION PICTURE

In 1970, singer Elvis Presley secretly met with President Richard Nixon. This new comedic novel imagines that Presley became a Central Intelligence Agency operative, eventually moving up through the ranks to become a skilled assassin.

Presented in an oral history fashion, the book tells us about Presley's secret transformation by the people who knew him best.

Did he fake his death in 1977? Was Presley involved with the Watergate scandal? The Iran hostage crisis? Communicating with aliens?

Read this book to find out the answers to these and many more questions.

Burning Bulb
PUBLISHING

MAD WORLD BY ANDY RAUSCH

"*Mad World* is dark, twisted, no-holds-barred fun."
—Jason Starr, author of *Bust*, *Slide*, and *The Max*

EVERYONE'S PLAYING AN ANGLE IN THE CITY OF ANGELS

Mad World tells the stories of a black hitman who doubles as a
university professor, a Catholic priest who longs to be a gangster,
a would-be author from Kansas, a gay phone sex operator who
claims he's straight, a group of rich twentysomethings playing a
deadly game of life and death, a vicious Mafia boss, and a sleazy
Hollywood movie director. As each of their stories intersect, the
body count piles up and the action comes nonstop in this tense,
white-knuckle thriller by first-time author Andy Rausch.

"A wild ride. If you like it gangster, *Mad World* delivers."
—Daniel Birch, author of *Get Some*

Burning Bulb
PUBLISHING

BLOODLETTING: A TALE OF REVENGE BY ANDY RAUSCH

"Relentless... Addictive... The kind of nightmare you don't want
to wake up from."
—Heywood Gould, screenwriter of *Rolling Thunder*

He was just an average Joe. But when he finds his family held at
gunpoint by merciless thugs, he's told he must murder a Mafia
chieftain if he ever wishes to see his loved ones again.

Against all odds, Joe keeps his end of the bargain, but the criminals
don't. Now at his wits end, Joe is pushed beyond his breaking point
and forced to exact bloody revenge against those who've done him
and his family wrong in this powerful and violent novella by author
Andy Rausch (*Mad World*).

"Andy Rausch has a tight noir style that combines gritty, realistic drama
with a cinematic flair that makes for a powerful, compelling (somewhat
Stephen Kingesque), authentically visual reading experience."
—Stephen Spignesi, author of *Dialogues*

Burning Bulb
PUBLISHING

THE TAILSMAN

From the creators of *The Big Book of Bizarro* and *Westward Hoes* comes a new comic unlike anything you have ever seen!

He's hot on the trail, looking for some *tail*...

Sly Franko was a man of the West, a forger of the wild frontier. Like the Country Western song that would be written years after he died, the words, "Faster horses, younger women, and more money," seemed to be the anthem of this horn dog cowboy.

Franko would ride into town on a blazing saddle, find the closest saloon to wet the whistle, belly up to a good card game, and find him a hot-loving hussy to get his cowpoke on with.

However, Sly might have met his match when a visit to bathroom leads to terror and death. Can Sly and his poker buddies solve the mystery before more of the townsfolk are murdered? Find out in this exciting premier issue of *The Tailsman!*

WWW.BURNINGBULBCOMICS.COM

THE HAGS OF BLACK COUNTY

by Michelle Bowser

Ruled by a committee of Hags, and fueled by toothless rivalries, Black County lurks just far enough out of the way to be completely unnoticed by the rest of civilization. Its inhabitants have been mentally warped for generations and the land itself seems to have the power to drive anyone unlucky enough to visit into ridiculous hillbilly madness. When a construction Company needs to bury a pipeline through its ludicrous hills and valleys, a twisted charm goes to work and every aspect of already bizarre Black County life takes a gory turn for the hysterical. Take a preposterous trip along with its citizens, both native and new, through escapades such as the Hag parade, the grand opening of Madame Skunk's House of Ill Repute, the demolition derby riot and the rabid, zombie clown apocalypse.

THE ABANDONED SOUL

by Daniel Sellers

After spending most of his 20s in a drug and alcohol fueled daze, a young man finally hits rock bottom. Having used up his friends and their good graces, he ends up squatting in an abandoned house. Forcibly sobering he begins to realize that he is not alone in this abandoned house. Left with one last friend and a mountain of regrets, he must decide if this presence is a guilty conscience, or a malicious hunter.

WE WISH YOU A HAPPY KILLDAY

by Jason Heroux

"We Wish You a Happy Killday" is the story of an international b eloved holiday called "Killday" where one day a year everyone over the age of fifteen is permitted to register for a license allowing them to kill one other person. But this year Chad Ovenstock doesn't feel like killing anyone. His friends and family urge him to participate in the festivities, but he can't seem to get into the holiday spirit. On the day before Killday Chad comes in contact with Ambrose, an old friend who suffered a nervous breakdown and is now part of The One Ant Army, a mysterious cult dedicated to making the future disappear. When the holiday finally arrives Chad refuses to participate and tries to survive on his own, surrounded by constant gunfire, countless corpses, and the nagging suspicion that Ambrose may have secretly brainwashed him into becoming a member of The One Ant Army cult.

Burning Bulb
PUBLISHING